S0-CCJ-310

"You're wrong, Mike," Leslie insisted. "It has not been my experience that people do crazy things when they're in love."

"People propose in front of millions of people at a ball game. They get married while skydiving. How can you say people in love aren't crazy?" he asked.

"People marry the boy next door, their high school sweetheart, or just because they have an urge to settle down, and they pick someone who feels the same way." She made a face. "That's not crazy behavior. In fact, it's very sensible."

"Don't you ever feel spontaneous, woman?" Mike exclaimed. "Love is the greatest emotion we have, not something you can take out and dust off because your neighbor is the opposite sex and right age. Molière says, 'Take love away from life and you take away its pleasures.' "

" '*What's Love Got to Do with It?*' Tina Turner," she shot back with a look that both teased and challenged.

"Everything," he said quickly. Then he pulled her into his arms—and he kissed her. Wildly, passionately, coaxingly.

Until Leslie surrendered to the irresistible seduction of his lips . . .

WHAT ARE *LOVESWEPT* ROMANCES?

They are stories of true romance and touching emotion. We believe those two very important ingredients are constants in our highly sensual and very believable stories in the LOVESWEPT *line. Our goal is to give you, the reader, stories of consistently high quality that may sometimes make you laugh, sometimes make you cry, but are always fresh and creative and contain many delightful surprises within their pages.*

Most romance fans read an enormous number of books. Those they truly love, they keep. Others may be traded with friends and soon forgotten. We hope that each LOVESWEPT *romance will be a treasure—a "keeper." We will always try to publish*

LOVE STORIES YOU'LL NEVER FORGET
BY AUTHORS YOU'LL ALWAYS REMEMBER

The Editors

IRRESISTIBLE STRANGER

LINDA CAJIO

BANTAM BOOKS

NEW YORK · TORONTO · LONDON · SYDNEY · AUCKLAND

IRRESISTIBLE STRANGER

A Bantam Book / December 1994

LOVESWEPT and the wave design are registered trademarks of Bantam Books, a division of Bantam Doubleday Dell Publishing Group, Inc. Registered in U.S. Patent and Trademark Office and elsewhere.

All rights reserved.
Copyright © 1994 by Linda Cajio.
Back cover art copyright © 1994 by Garin Baker.
Floral border by Lori Nelson Field.
No part of this book may be reproduced or transmitted in any form or by any means, electronic or mechanical, including photocopying, recording, or by any information storage and retrieval system, without permission in writing from the publisher.
For information address: Bantam Books.

If you purchased this book without a cover you should be aware that this book is stolen property. It was reported as "unsold and destroyed" to the publisher and neither the author nor the publisher has received any payment for this "stripped book."

If you would be interested in receiving protective vinyl covers for your Loveswept books, please write to this address for information:

Loveswept
Bantam Books
P.O. Box 985
Hicksville, NY 11802

ISBN 0-553-44276-7

Published simultaneously in the United States and Canada

Bantam Books are published by Bantam Books, a division of Bantam Doubleday Dell Publishing Group, Inc. Its trademark, consisting of the words "Bantam Books" and the portrayal of a rooster, is Registered in U.S. Patent and Trademark Office and in other countries. Marca Registrada. Bantam Books, 1540 Broadway, New York, New York 10036.

PRINTED IN THE UNITED STATES OF AMERICA

OPM 0 9 8 7 6 5 4 3 2 1

Many thanks to E.P. for the inspiration.

PROLOGUE

"I can't believe I'm going to England! This is so exciting!"

"I just hope this morning flight leaves at ten-fifteen like it's supposed to. After being up most of the night, I know I'll sleep my way over. . . ."

The voices caught the man's attention, and he immediately gravitated toward the two women speaking. One was tall and thin, the other shorter and plumper, but both were in their late twenties or early thirties and looked exactly like what they were. Tourists. Even better, the plump one held a small carry-on bag that was identical to his own. No special straps with her name on it; no fancy identity tags; no betraying scuff marks. Just a brand-new blue Samsonite, of which there were millions in use and, doubtless, one or two others on the flight from Kennedy to London. He'd banked on that . . . banked on the mass confusion that always reigned at one of the busiest airports in the world.

All it would take would be one little switch and "The Adams" would go across the pond, easy as pie—and without ever being traced back to him.

With all the airport security measures for bombs and drugs, he couldn't take the chance of carrying the materials himself. Of course that security was a blessing, since he was reasonably assured his merchandise wouldn't be blown up. But still, he couldn't take it over himself.

He got into the security check line at the edge of the terminal right behind the women, hoping to make the switch on the other side, where all the bags tended to pile together after going through the X-ray machine. The taller woman, however, set her distinctively different bag in between his and the other. The man cursed at the lost opportunity.

And then the taller woman laughed.

The laugh caught his attention in an entirely different way. It was deep and throaty, sending a shiver of animal magnetism down the man's spine, making him want to hear it again. In bed. After making love.

He caught hold of himself, knowing it was a mistake to have a feeling for his victim or his victim's traveling companion. That wouldn't do at all.

The tall one, still laughing that wonderful

laugh, said, "I remember the last time you had a premonition that a man was coming into your life, Gerry. You found a male kitten the next day."

"Was I wrong?" his target asked triumphantly. "I have it on this trip. And I have it for you, Leslie."

The woman scoffed as she walked through the metal detector.

The man smiled slightly at the woman security guard as he passed through the detector himself. Out of the corner of his eye he watched his bag on the X-ray screen. It was packed with the usual toiletries and other ordinary paraphernalia any passenger would need.

Even down to "The Adams."

He didn't miss his next opportunity when the tall woman went into the ladies' room and the plump one named Gerry walked into the nearly empty gift shop. Lovely woman that Gerry obviously was, she set her bag down on the floor while she paid for her magazines and Life Savers. He set his down right next to hers, stretching his fingers as if the bag was heavy.

"I know how you feel," she murmured to him. "Mine weighs a ton too."

He hoped not. Smiling at her, he said, "Know what you mean."

He picked up a newspaper, set exact change on the counter, then picked up a bag and turned toward the entrance, not rushing, but hurrying as if he were concerned about the time he had left until his flight took off. On his way out he passed Gerry's tall companion coming into the shop. She never even blinked at him.

He headed for the rest room and occupied a stall for a time—enough to allow the women to get to their gate, hopefully without noticing the bag. The identity tag with its wonderful cover flap was the manufacturer's original. He pushed up the flap and read the information with great satisfaction. When he emerged from the men's room, he strolled down the terminal walkway and past the waiting lounge for the departure gate the women would be using. They were there already and so was the bag, settled nicely against the one woman's leg.

Smiling to himself, he went to the nearest bank of telephones and dialed a number. When the other end was answered, he said, "Gerry O'Hanlon. American Air. Flight Six-four-three."

The Adams was on its way.

ONE

She would shoot Gerry O'Hanlon the moment she saw her again.

Leslie Marie Kloslosky threw her purse and overnighter on the one twin bed, glared at the other, then kicked it, furious with her companion. Gerry had taken her own premonition about romance seriously—again—and flirted with the man in the seat next to her for the entire seven-hour flight. She'd walked off the plane and literally into the sunset with the guy, with an airy "I'll catch up" tossed in Leslie's direction.

"I'll catch up, my backside," Leslie muttered, very frustrated with one of her oldest friends.

She and Gerry had planned this trip for months, the vacation to end all vacations. Yes, Gerry could be flaky at times—that was the fun of being her friend—but she'd never been so irresponsible before. Never like this.

The only thing Leslie could point a finger to was Gerry's growing fear of getting older and remaining single. Thirty-three was hardly old, yet despite having gone through a marriage and divorce, Leslie couldn't help the occasional stab of panic at the thought of being alone in her old age. Still, that didn't excuse Gerry running out on her like this. She'd even stuck Leslie with her luggage!

Leslie scowled at the blue carry-on bag and bigger matching suitcase. She should have dumped the damn things at the airport Lost and Found and let Gerry claim them. It would serve her right.

Leslie's stomach growled, reminding her that she'd slept her way across the Atlantic and missed several meals. Now it was *way* past her dinnertime. She decided to find the dining room, rather than wait for Gerry. Besides, Gerry would probably go out to dinner with the man. Leslie had to admit he seemed nice enough, like a nondescript bookkeeper, but she hoped Gerry hadn't lost all common sense.

The Columbia Hotel was wonderfully Old World British, with narrow corridors and a narrower lift. Leslie squeezed herself into the elevator, wondering how she'd gotten in the first time with all the luggage. No one else could fit, surely. In fact it made her nervous to be in the tiny box. Maybe five flights of stairs wouldn't be so bad.

The staircase was all marble and red carpet, really beautiful. . . .

The doors began to close before she could change her mind, but two hands shoved at them suddenly, forcing them open again. A tall man got in, taking up all the extra space—and all the air.

"Nearly didn't make it," he said in a true-blue American accent.

Leslie stared at him. She couldn't help herself. He was so tall, he had to hunch over in the lift. His haircut had long grown out, and his thick dark hair brushed the collar of his oxford button-down shirt and tan jacket. He was thin, truly thin, not wiry or compact, which only accentuated his height. The bones of his face stood out sharply, almost harshly. It was easy to envision him as a brooding, commanding man—except for his glasses. The round, tortoiseshell frames softened his features just enough to make one think of a college professor. A strict one, maybe. His blue eyes certainly didn't have a gentle look; they were too light in color for that.

A sure feeling came over her, like knowing when she pulled a dress off a clothing rack that it would fit perfectly and look wonderful. Just a sense of positive awareness mixed in with the overwhelming sensual one. Like a premonition.

Leslie forced away the notion. Premonitions were Gerry's territory, not hers.

The doors finished closing. They hung in space for a long moment, then a bang sounded somewhere above them and the lift began to descend, creaking loudly. Leslie could feel the scream rising inside her, but she refused to panic. If she had no chance of bursting through to safety, she owed it to her fellow lift passenger to keep her hysteria to herself.

An awkward silence ensued as the lift traveled down to the lobby. Leslie knew she ought to say something, but she couldn't find her tongue. She was practically crouched back against the far wall. A coffin had to be bigger, she thought, then berated herself for the morbid idea. But she wondered what his seat mate on his flight had done for space. This was like being locked in with Jeffrey Giraffe.

A sexy Jeffrey Giraffe, she amended, for her awareness level was clocking in at light speed. The very air between them seemed charged.

He didn't appear hot and bothered, however. Instead he took out a pipe and clamped it between his teeth, then patted his pockets, clearly searching for tobacco and matches.

Leslie gasped at the idea of him actually smoking a pipe in the lift. He couldn't be serious. One puff and the air in there wouldn't pass even the EPA's most lenient rules. She coughed in dreaded anticipation of his lighting up.

He glanced at her, then blinked as if he'd forgotten anyone else was in the squeeze box with him. He took the pipe out of his mouth and put it back in his pocket. She sighed in relief.

The lift doors opened, and clearly wanting to be mannerly, he waved her out first.

She looked at the three-inch margin between him and the doors and decided she could make it.

It was a mistake.

She tried her best to press herself into the lift's front wall, but her derriere still brushed along his pelvis and thighs.

"Oh, Lord," she muttered under her breath, mortified to be touching a stranger in such an intimate manner. Worse, her blood was heating in a way that had nothing to do with embarrassment and everything to do with sensuality.

It couldn't be instant attraction, she thought, desperately resisting the overwhelming urge to press back against the man. Instant attraction was for Gerry, not for her. She had always been sane and sensible. Mothers had allowed their daughters to go places and do things with her "because Leslie's such a sensible girl." Even in marriage she'd been sane and sensible. That was why Jim had left her for a more exciting woman. So what was happening now was ridiculous. Sane and sensible women did not have instant attractions for strangers they met on vacation. They settled for sane and sensible sex with safe men.

Nonetheless something very unsane and unsensible was happening to her. But *he* didn't seem be having the same problem. He simply stood still and waited patiently for her to move past him and on out of the lift.

10

Her instant attraction shriveled into instant humiliation.

Leslie extricated herself from the lift in record time. Her hands were shaking as she practically raced through the lobby. Her head spun, and she felt as if she were back on the elevator, because her body seemed to be going up and down of its own accord.

Jet lag, she told herself. She wasn't having a bout of instant attraction, she was suffering from good old jet lag.

The dining room was empty, and a waitress was clearing up the last of the tables. Leslie sagged against the brightly painted molding, her stomach so empty that she felt slightly queasy. She knew if she didn't eat soon, she'd have a migraine headache. It always happened when she was low on food and water.

"I'm sorry," the waitress said, catching sight of her. "The dining room is closed now."

"Please," she said, willing to beg for a meal if she had to. "I've just gotten off the plane from the States and I'm starving. I don't want to be any trouble, but couldn't someone make bacon and eggs or something? Anything really. Cereal and milk. A sandwich. A stale roll. Bad lettuce. I'll eat anything. I'll pay double."

The woman frowned, unsure for a moment, then smiled and waved her in. "Chef hasn't left yet, so I'll see what I can do for you and your husband."

"Husband?" Leslie glanced around to see the man from the lift closing the last few feet between them. The waitress had clearly assumed because he was heading in the direction of the dining room, he was with her. She turned back, saying, "He's not my husband."

"Oh," the waitress said. "Well, whatever."

"But—"

"Thank you," the man said. He had a pleasant voice, not too deep, but not high-pitched either.

"But—" Leslie tried again, as the waitress hustled through the swinging doors to the kitchen.

Her lift companion took her arm, his touch sending off those disconcerting sparks again. Her body had a second reaction, like the one when she'd had to move past him, not as sharp, but slower and deeper. She tried to regain her breath as he guided her toward a table for two.

"If she thinks we're separate," he said, "she may not serve either of us, so bear with me, okay? I can't afford to lose a meal, believe me."

"I do," she said, her voice cracking in ominous betrayal. Gerry couldn't be right, she thought. Gerry? Right? That was like the moon hurtling down to the earth.

She wondered if the whooshing noise in her ears *was* the moon hurtling down to the earth, then realized it was the blood rushing in her ears. The world tilted a little before righting itself again. She couldn't be having this kind of reaction to a man—like hot, heavy, unexpected sex, overwhelming her senses. Not her. Not Leslie Kloslosky.

Once they were seated and facing each other, she forced herself to relax. Unfortunately her gaze couldn't seem to settle on his face. She'd look, then look away again, terrified he'd see the jumbled feelings inside her.

Get a grip, woman! she told herself. She tried to smile, but felt as if her upper lip was sticking to her teeth, giving her a Bugs Bunny look. It was Gerry and her damn premonitions, she thought. The notion had been put in her head, and now her body was running with it. He didn't seem to notice, and she didn't know whether she ought to be grateful or take him out and shoot him.

He said, "You're American. So am I. Mike Smith from Philly." He grinned. "Somebody has to be."

"Watch it. I grew up in Roxborough," she said, naming a neighborhood of the city. Words had actually come out of her mouth, coherently and firmly. She was proud of herself. "I'm Leslie Kloslosky."

"Small world, Leslie Kloslosky."

She nodded, wondering again if Gerry's premonition was really right, then dismissing the thought. Americans could be found in every major city in Europe, probably in every decent hotel too. Why should she be surprised? Even the Philadelphia connection was sheer coincidence, not destiny, fate, karma, kismet, and all that other hocus-pocus romance stuff. She was thirty-three, divorced, been around the block upon occasion and certainly knew better. She just wished her body would pay attention to that fact.

"This is a lovely old hotel," Mike said, taking off his glasses. He began to polish them with his napkin.

"Beautiful," she agreed. She watched the delicate way his fingers slowly smoothed the linen cloth around and around the lens.

"I've stayed here several times," he continued. "It's got an Old World charm, don't you think?"

"Yes," she said, then realized her end of the conversation thus far had been less than brilliant. Tarzan could have done better. She dragged her gaze away from his hands, adding, "It's my first time here, but I'm glad my agent didn't book the Hilton."

"The chains are fine, but they don't give you a feel for the country the way independent hotels do."

"But you do know what you're getting with them, no matter where you are."

They were clicking, she thought. She didn't want to click. She was only here for two days, and she'd never had or been a one-night stand in her life. Now was not the time to start—no matter how attracted she was.

The waitress returned. "You're in luck.

Chef'll do you bacon and eggs. Would you like coffee?"

"Tea for me," Mike said. He looked expectantly at her.

"Coffee will be fine."

So he drank tea, she thought. So much for those commercials where the sexy guy was always borrowing coffee from his woman neighbor and inviting her to Paris. Oh, Leslie, she told herself again, get a grip.

He put his pipe in his mouth and patted his pockets, then stared at her for a long moment. He took the pipe out of his mouth, but fiddled with it, turning it in his hands.

Leslie watched those hands with even greater fascination than before. They were overly large and awkward-looking. He could probably snap the pipe in two without effort. Yet the fingers were long and slim, and she wondered what they would feel like skimming over a woman's body.

Her body . . .

He stuck the pipe back in his mouth but didn't light it.

Heat suffusing her face, Leslie forced herself to concentrate on nothing at all. Maybe talking would help.

"Have you been here long?" she asked.

He frowned. "No, I came down with you, remember?"

"No. I mean, in England."

"Ahh . . . in England. Not long. You?"

"I just arrived today." And she was ready to go home again. No friend. No common sense. She never should have gotten out of bed that morning. Whenever that had been.

"You look . . . unhappy," he said.

"Oh, no," she said hastily, dismayed that her problems must have shown on her face. She might be attracted to him, but she wasn't about to spill her guts. She could feel heat flushing her cheeks. "I'm fine, just tired. I had an early-morning flight out."

"Not the usual night flight?" he asked, raising his eyebrows. "Most people take the night flight to be oriented to the new time zone."

Leslie bristled. She'd had the same argument from everyone—except her travel agent. "It makes more sense to arrive at night when you're tired, then you can go straight to bed and get on local time right away. But if you arrive in the morning, you have to stay up all day to orient yourself. That seemed like sheer torture to me."

He shrugged. "I always sleep on the flight over, so I'm wide awake when I get here."

"I slept, too, on the flight over—"

"Then you ought to be wide awake now. See? You should have taken the night flight."

Leslie set her teeth together. Obviously he didn't get the point and it would be a waste of time to belabor it. And if anyone knew about wasting time, it was a time management consultant, and that was she.

The waitress arrived with their coffee and tea. Leslie took a healthy sip of hers. The flavor was slightly different, but that didn't detract from the mental snap-into-place that coffee always gave her. She felt better immediately, then wondered if she'd be up all night. That Mike Smith might actually be right about her taking a differently timed flight was disturbing. She'd planned this trip sensibly—or had, until Gerry had taken a curve on her. Gerry always did the unexpected—that was the fun of having her for a friend—but this time she was being downright irresponsible.

Leslie frowned. She could spend the whole trip sulking and waste her money, not to mention her time. Gerry was just having dinner with a man she met. She was entitled, after all.

And that's all it had better be, Leslie thought.

Mike poured his tea and took a sip. "So are you with a tour?"

"Yes and no." Her body shot up three floors, then back down again, thanks to the coffee's temporary effect against the jet lag. She pressed her fingers to her temple, saying, "We . . . I . . . we meet with one in Shropshire."

"Ahh . . . *A Country Lad.* 'In valleys of springs and rivers. By Ony and Teme and Clun . . .' "

"I beg your pardon?"

Mike stared at her as if she'd lost her wits. "A. E. Housman. The poet. He immortalized Shropshire in his works."

"Oh. Actually I'm going to see the abbey at Shrewsbury." He frowned in puzzlement, so she prompted, naming a popular fictional detective series, her personal favorite. "Brother Alaric, medieval detective monk . . . Elias Peterson, the author . . ."

"Never heard of them."

Leslie could feel that heat coming back in her face. She was positive she'd blushed more times with this man in a half hour than she ever had in her entire teenage years. Why should she be embarrassed that she was going to see the real-life setting for a series of books she admired? It wasn't a mortal sin, for goodness' sake. But it proved one thing. She and Mr. Instant Attraction had about as much in common as a wolf and a carburetor. And he didn't have to make it sound as if it were beneath him to read mysteries.

The waitress came with dinner, laying their plates before them. Leslie looked at her meal, limply garnished with two halves of grilled tomato. The bacon was familiar, but the sunny-side-up eggs had strange deeply-colored orange yolks. Her stomach did the elevator flip again, but it wasn't from jet lag this time.

Mike was already cutting his meal up with relish, spearing bacon pieces along with egg.

I can't, I can't, she thought, closing her eyes.

"I thought you were starving to death," he commented.

"I am."

She knew if she didn't try to eat, she'd be in worse trouble. She started with the bacon, and her stomach returned to normal—growling with demands. By the time she got to the eggs, she was prepared to deal with them. Like the coffee, they were slightly different but not bad. At least her stomach didn't fully rebel. Mike didn't say anything. He just ate.

Michael Jack Smith watched his companion out of the corner of his eye. Leslie Kloslosky wasn't the kind of woman to whom he was normally attracted. She was far too tall, for one thing. He preferred his women smaller, an incongruity that hadn't escaped him on several uncomfortable occasions. But Leslie . . . well, there was something different about Leslie.

Her features weren't striking at first, and she had a no-nonsense look about her, but contradictory details came to the forefront the longer one observed her. Her eyebrows curved perfectly over eyes the color of the sea on a clear day, giving her a knowing look. Her skin was creamy, paler than one expected for a brunette, and she had a sprinkling of freckles, the last remnants of girlhood that would never quite fade away. Her lips were full—if she would allow them to be. Right now they were thinned as she concentrated on eating. Her breasts rose and fell slowly with her every breath. Under her shirt he could see the tips tilted upward, causing his blood to pound along his veins. The rest of her he knew was slender. She was graceful, not sassy in her movements. He'd watched her enough to know that already. And what she did to a man's senses . . .

He'd nearly come undone in that dinky lift when she'd slid by him to get out. He would have shamed himself and scared her half to death if he had. Just looking at her caused things to go off inside him.

"How's the food?" he asked, knowing if he stared at her any longer without talking, he'd make an idiot of himself. He had a feeling she didn't suffer fools gladly.

"Different from the States, but all right."

Typical tourist, he thought in amusement. They always wanted everything the same as home. Why bother to travel if they weren't willing to find new experiences? " *'Dis-moi ce que tu manges, je te dirai ce que tu es.'* "

She stared at him in bewilderment. "I beg your pardon?"

" 'Tell me what you eat, and I will tell you what you are,' " he repeated in English. "Brillat-Savarin said that. He's considered by some to be the greatest chef who ever lived."

"I thought he was a coffee." She shrugged. "Okay, so I'm dull and American. I can accept that."

"You wouldn't want the same old thing in another country, surely. The charm is eating what the natives eat."

"My stomach isn't so sure about that."

He chuckled at her rueful tone. "It'll adjust. Trust me."

"Last time I heard that, my mother was about to dose me with cod liver oil."

He laughed, liking her wry sense of humor. Still, he knew the attraction was a distraction he didn't need at the moment. It had taken some fancy talking for him to get his sabbatical, and he shouldn't waste it.

When the check came several minutes later, Leslie realized she was in trouble. She hadn't changed over her money yet. She supposed she could sign the meal off to her room, but after all the effort the waitress had gone to on her behalf, it seemed tacky not to leave the tip right at the table. Maybe Mike would be a gentleman and pay it. . . .

Looking up, she found him in the throes of patting pockets again and pulling out change from everywhere, stacking the coins on the table. It was obvious that the man was about as organized as a flock of pigeons with a cat in the middle of it. More evidence that Gerry's premonition had gone bust with this one.

He would drive a time management consultant crazy in two hours.

"Give me your half of the bill," she said, holding out her hand.

He stopped in the middle of unwrapping a wadded-up five-pound note. "What?"

"I don't have English cash yet. Give me your share and I'll sign off for the meal."

"Why should you sign off for the whole meal?"

"Because I don't have cash yet," she repeated.

"What does that have to do with anything?"

"I want to leave a tip for the waitress and *not* bill that to my room. That would be tacky. So give me your half, and I can leave a tip."

"But what about my tip?"

He was genuinely puzzled. She wondered if words penetrated whatever fog surrounded him. It must be the pipe smoke.

"I will leave your tip with my tip." She smiled sweetly, her hand still outstretched. If he didn't hand over the money in the next three seconds, she decided she'd strangle that long neck of his. She wondered what the British penalty was for murder at the dinner table.

"I see," he said. "Actually I don't, but here."

He shoved the money across the linen tablecloth. Leslie signed the bill, along with leaving her room number, piled the money neatly to the side, then rose from her seat.

"Hey! You're leaving the whole thing!" His voice boomed across the room.

"Yes," she hissed, mortified that they might be overheard. "She deserves it for all the extra trouble she went to for us. Now, will you get up from the damn table!"

"Boy, you are from Philadelphia." But he got

up from the table and followed her out of the room.

He was still with her as they crossed the lobby. Leslie groaned to herself, amazed that she'd even considered him as a "possible." He was an impossible. Yes, he was nice, but that was about it. They had absolutely nothing in common. Nothing. It was just as well she'd be in London for such a short time. How long would Mike be in the city? she wondered. Was he on vacation too?

"Are you on vacation?" she asked, then cursed her curiosity getting the better of her. She wasn't supposed to be interested. Unfortunately the rest of her was having trouble assimilating that.

"No," he answered. "I teach English Lit at Temple University. Right now I'm on a sabbatical to study the works of Ben Jonson."

"Figures."

"What does that mean?" he asked.

"Nothing." She grinned. "Well . . . you *are* the absentminded professor, aren't you?"

"I am?"

"You are."

They squeezed into the tiny elevator again. Leslie suppressed the sudden, sharp remembrances of their last ride. Opposites might attract, but they certainly weren't what relationships were made of.

"I'm not absentminded . . ." Clearly Mike

had been chewing on her words. ". . . And you've only known me for five minutes, so how can you say that?"

She smiled. "It's more like thirty minutes. And that's all it takes sometimes."

"But I never miss a class. I'm always on time for dentist appointments, and I hate them. That's hardly absentminded. Anyway, what do you do?"

"I'm a time management counselor."

"Now, *that* figures."

"And what does that mean?" she demanded.

He smiled smugly. The doors opened and he stepped through them, saying, "Like you said, it only takes a few minutes sometimes."

She stepped out after him. Charged through was more like it, but she didn't care. He had a nerve, she thought, making her sound like some kind of fussy old maid. Fortunately he was heading in the same direction as her room, so she could walk with him without being conspicuous.

"I'm occasionally late for hair appointments," she said in her defense. "I hate housekeeping, so I don't do it. And I believe in live-and-let-live as long as one doesn't hurt anybody. So how can you imply that I'm some rigid clock watcher?"

"You do have very set notions of things, such as tips."

"And you don't understand anything logical."

"You eat very precisely. First all the bacon, then all the eggs. It was like watching a surgeon."

She didn't answer him. Instead she was staring ahead at the figure at the end of the corridor fiddling with the doorknob of a room.

"Hey!" she exclaimed. "That's my room!"

TWO

Mike wondered if an absentminded professor would spin around in circles like an idiot rather than instantly take off down the corridor to tackle the intruder. He ran like hell anyway, his long strides eating up the carpet.

The intruder, eyes wide under a ski mask, turned on his heel and pounded down the corridor. Mike ran faster. The guy made a sharp right and seemingly disappeared into the wall. Mike reached it several seconds later to discover the man had gone down a back stairwell. He hit the door, bursting it open, then skidded to a halt, listening for whether the intruder had gone up or down. Not hearing a thing, he chose down as the most logical way an escaping criminal would go.

And she said he wasn't logical.

A short time later he discovered criminals weren't logical, because his hadn't come this way.

The stairs emptied out into the kitchen area. He questioned the few people still cleaning up, but no one had seen anything. As he climbed the stairs back up to the fifth floor, he checked every floor, but the intruder had long vanished. Mike had to admit he'd blown his chance of catching the man and impressing Leslie. He only hoped there would be others.

"Well?" Leslie asked, when he arrived back on her floor. "Did you catch him?"

"No." He refrained from pointing out that the man would be in tow if he had. Logic was her department, after all. "I suppose you ought to go report this."

She raised her eyebrows. "No kidding."

He grit his teeth, wondering why he was bothering. But he knew perfectly well why. Her long legs were a major attraction all on their own. Usually his six feet six inches ensured that he was continually hunched over a woman, like a father with a child. With Leslie Kloslosky, he was nearly eye-to-eye, as nearly as he'd ever get. She had to be at least five feet ten inches tall in her stocking feet. With heels, she'd be a knockout. He had the urge, even now, to undo the band at her nape and run his fingers through her thick, shoulder-length tresses. She'd fit him, every inch, everywhere. He was positive of it. Although he wasn't one to just pick a woman up, he couldn't pass her by. It was as if fate, destiny, kismet, providence—all those good words—were at work here.

"Better check your room," he suggested, "just to be sure he was in the process of getting in, not going out."

Her mouth opened in a perfect O of astonishment, then she whirled around and fumbled with her key and the doorknob, finally getting it open. Mike peeked in as she entered. He tried to keep his focus on finding anything that looked suspicious, but he kept being distracted by her bending over as she searched through her things. She had a great—

She mumbled something.

He blinked. "I beg your pardon?"

"I said my stuff looks okay, but I can't be sure about Gerry's."

"Gerry?" It sounded like a man's name. Dammit.

She nodded. "My friend. We're on this trip together. Or we're supposed to be."

He frowned, not liking the word *friend*. "You sound as if something happened to him."

Leslie straightened and shrugged. "Her. She's out to dinner with a friend tonight. I can't get inside her luggage, but everything looks secure. If you'll excuse me—"

"Oh, sure." He stepped away from the threshold reluctantly, relieved that Gerry was a woman. Not an hour ago the most exciting thing he could think of was getting his hands on the original manuscript of the play *Sejanus* by Jonson, housed at Cambridge University. The script was priceless, and he'd been dying to see it. The margins actually had Jonson's notes to Shakespeare, who was supposed to have been a member of the cast. Incredible. But Leslie Kloslosky had come along, throwing him off balance. He didn't like that, especially now when he needed his concentration so badly for his new thesis. It was a publish-or-perish world in academia, and he needed to publish something soon or he would lose his standing in the department.

She locked the door behind her and began walking down the corridor. He followed her.

She stopped and turned around. "What are you doing?"

He frowned. "I'm going with you."

"Why? Oh, thank you for chasing the burglar."

"You're welcome. Because you're going to report the attempted break-in. I'm a witness. And I chased him, remember?"

"Oh." She really did have beautiful eyes. A man could lose himself in their depths.

He waved a hand. "Shall we go to the elevator?"

The thought made him grin.

Normally Leslie would have been thrilled to have been inside New Scotland Yard. Normally.

She trudged out the front doors of the famous police building, just as the first gray streaks of dawn lighted the eastern sky. Granted, she was upset, but she never would have thought an attempted break-in would garner so many questions and forms to be filled out. No wonder the Yard was so good, she thought. They hammered their witnesses into the ground for clues.

And then there was the waiting. She and Mike had spent more time on a bench than in an office. She'd felt like a ball player being punished for losing the last game.

"That was interesting," Mike said from behind her.

His cheerful voice grated on her frazzled nerves. He seemed to take all the fuss in stride. In fact he'd grown more enthusiastic as the night wore on.

"Of course it's interesting!" she snapped. "*You* don't have jet lag, and you're obviously a night person. I'm not."

"You're tired."

She whirled on him, wondering just how obtuse he was. How could he *not* recognize that she was exhausted—beyond exhausted? Talk about absentminded . . . She forced herself to calm down, realizing how sarcastic she'd sounded. "I'm sorry. You're right, though, I am tired."

"I'll get us a lift home." He went back into the building, leaving her standing on the sidewalk.

"Wonderful," she muttered, feeling abandoned. Then she wondered why she was fussing.

Hadn't she wanted to get away from him? He scared her. Not physically, but every time he was within two feet of her, her emotional and sexual equilibrium swung around the dial. Now was her opportunity, and here she was, wasting it as she mentally bitched about him.

She began walking down the street, uniformed and plainclothes men and women passing her on their way into the building. Yawning, she promised herself to return at another time, when she could appreciate things better. She was halfway down the block when she realized she didn't know where she was going. And there was no cab in sight.

"Great," she muttered, disgusted with herself. If she had known all this would happen, she would have pulled the covers back over her head yesterday—

Good Lord, was it only yesterday that she was home in Jersey?

"Hey! I told you to wait. Don't you listen?"

Mike was leaning out the back window of a police car that was driving slowly alongside her. She stopped. It stopped.

"Yes, I listen," she said.

"Then what are you doing here?"

"Taking a morning constitutional."

"I thought you were tired."

She walked over to the car and got in next to him, keeping as much space as possible between them. Even in her exhaustion her awareness of him went up a notch and her heart pounded a bit faster. The attraction was so strong that although she was tired and angry, she was still responding to it. This *had* to stop.

"Thank you," she said to the driver.

"You're welcome, miss. You want to be careful crossing outside the striped crosswalks. If a car hits you, he's in the right."

Leslie stared at the back of the bobby's head. "Really? Pedestrians don't have the right of way here?"

"Only at the crosswalks and only at the ones with flashing lights. Not that a chap likes to run someone over, you understand. Makes a mess of the car."

"Not to mention the person," Mike commented. "I don't think Leslie would like that."

Leslie said nothing. After a few minutes of strained silence she realized she was being an ass again. How did Mike manage to do that with her? The idea of predestiny seemed even more ludicrous when the man involved was able to get the woman to act foolishly on a regular basis. She cleared her throat. "Thank you, Mike, for getting us a lift back. I'm grateful not to have to walk."

"It didn't make any sense when we've been good tourists and they have the cars."

"I feel bad for you," she admitted. "You strolled along into this. It wasn't even your room that was nearly broken into."

He grinned. "One strolls through life and one gets unexpected rewards."

She wasn't sure he was talking about a night's adventure in Scotland Yard, but she wasn't about to inquire either. *If one does not ask, one can live happily in ignorance—Leslie Kloslosky.*

At the hotel she couldn't get to her room fast enough, her weariness compounding itself with each step. The first thing she'd do, she promised herself, was to fall fully dressed into her bed. Right smack onto the mattress and sleep all day. It didn't matter that she'd screw up her inner clock. It was probably irreparable by now. She was so tired, she was about three doors from promised paradise when she realized Mike was still walking with her.

She stopped. "Where are you going?"

"To your room."

She gaped at him. He looked at her expectantly. "You can't!" she exclaimed.

"Why not?"

"Why?"

"Because your room should be checked. Maybe the burglar came back while you were gone."

She gaped at him again. "Oh, Lord, no! I couldn't take a whole *day* at the Yard!"

She hurried down the hall to her door, getting it open in record time. Everything was in place from last night. Or at least everything looked that way. To Leslie's consternation the only thing missing was Gerry herself.

"Better check," Mike said.

With a groan she began going through her things, vowing she'd never read a police procedural mystery again. Real life was not suspenseful, just plain old tedious. She knew that now. Her bed looked so inviting. She forced herself to ignore it, but the battle was a losing one. She was just about to tell Mike to go away, and to sink into the covers, when the telephone rang.

"Hi! It's me," Gerry said as soon as Leslie answered it.

"Dammit, Gerry! Where are you?" she demanded.

"In bed. Oh, what a lovely man—"

"You just met him, for goodness' sake!"

"But it was kismet, Leslie." Gerry's voice was hurt.

Leslie stared up at the ceiling, trying to grab on to her patience, what little there was of it. She didn't want to explode in anger in front of Mike, who was standing by the dresser, looking studiously at the wall. She turned her back on him and in a low voice said, "I hope you're playing it safe—if you know what I mean."

"I haven't completely lost my mind."

Leslie sighed. "Emotionally too."

"Yes, Mama."

"The room was nearly broken into last night."

"Oh, no! Are you okay?"

"I'm fine. He only got as far as trying the door." Leslie told her about it, leaving out one big detail. Mike. She finished with, "I've just checked again, and everything's okay. Except for your luggage. But the bags don't look tampered with, so they ought to be okay too. I'll probably be asleep when you get here—"

"I . . . I'm not coming."

Leslie was positive her ears were having a jet-lag reaction. She couldn't have heard right. "What did you say?"

"I'll meet you in Cornwall. I feel really badly about this, Leslie, but I hope you won't mind. Well, at least understand. Tully wants me to stay. He's wonderful, Leslie. The most special man. It's just for a few days more. I'm in love."

Leslie sank down on the bed, oblivious of its enticement to sleep. "I don't believe this."

"I don't blame you for being mad. I know it's a rotten thing to do, but I can't help myself. I *have* to be with him. When you fall in love, you'll understand."

Mike coughed.

Leslie closed her eyes against the world. She couldn't face it all at the moment without killing someone. Never had the urge to hit something been so overwhelming. Finally she said the only thing that came into her mind. "But the hair dryer's in your bag."

"Oh, thank you, thank you for not hating me

for life," Gerry said with clearly heartfelt gratitude. "No problem about the dryer. I keep the spare key for each bag in its outside compartment."

"Gerry!" Leslie exclaimed, horrified by this latest display of laissez-faire traveling.

"Well, if I lose the other key, how can I get into my suitcases? It makes sense to keep one right on the bag."

"You're incredible. And you'd damn well better be in Cornwall!"

"I promise, I promise. Leslie, you're a peach."

When Gerry hung up, Leslie decided there was a poetic injustice in Gerry getting the man and her getting the hair dryer. She turned to face Mike, who had finally left off examining the wallpaper. He blinked owlishly from behind his glasses, and she wondered if he had only been polite or had really been interested in the wallpaper.

"That was Gerry," she said.

"So I gather."

"She's . . . staying with a friend for a while."

He nodded.

Clearing her throat, she stood up and went to the door, holding it open. "Since the room checks out, I'd really like to catch up on some sleep."

"Oh."

He walked over to the door, put his hand on the outside knob, then stopped to face her. "If you have any problems . . . if you hear anything strange, call me at my room. Five-twenty-four."

"I'll call security," she said sensibly.

He leaned forward, his face scant inches from hers. "And call me."

"Oh, no—"

"Call me."

His concern touched her. They might not be at all compatible, but he did have a gentlemanly streak. She smiled her thanks, afraid to say anything because of the sudden lump of tears in her throat.

He closed the space between them and settled his lips on hers. Leslie's head reeled at the warmth of his mouth, at the taste of him, soft yet virile. The kiss was gentle, but it was like touching off live wires. The sparks flew in unexpected showers inside her. His mouth moved against hers in a seductive rhythm, causing her head to spin even more. He was leaning over her, even as she was on tiptoe. It was a wonderful feeling to have to reach up for a kiss. Usually she was eye-to-eye with a man, or even inconspicuously trying to make herself smaller.

She moved into the kiss, wanting more. He pulled her into his embrace, slanting his lips across hers in sudden demand. Their tongues swirled together in a sensual duel that made her forget everything but the touch of his mouth and body against hers. His fingers spread low across her waist, pressing her intimately to him. She wrapped her arms around his shoulders, digging her nails into his jacket, trying to hang on to a piece of sanity against the sensations rocking through her.

Sensibility seemed like such a silly thing compared with the onslaught of his kiss. Premonition, however, was more than a possibility. It was downright absolute.

He finally eased his mouth away, then eased her out of his embrace. "Get some sleep, Leslie. Before I forget myself."

He slipped out the door, closing it so quietly behind him that it seemed to float into place on its own.

Leslie sank back against the wood, shocked at her reaction to him. How could someone who was so wrong for her kiss so right? She looked down to see if she still had her socks on and was further shocked to find they weren't. Then she remembered she was wearing stockings.

Maybe a good long sleep would clear her head. She *was* at less than one hundred percent, after all. The sooner she got rid of the jet lag, the better.

This bout was a doozy.

"I thought you were supposed to be asleep."

Leslie stared up at Mike from her corner table in the hotel dining room, then looked away. Only a few hours ago he had left her in her room to catch up on her sleep. He had also left her dazed and bewildered from that kiss.

"I was hungry," she said lamely, by way of explanation. She wasn't about to tell him that his kiss had kept her nerve endings sizzling for a long time after he'd left. She had decided that if she couldn't sleep, she could at least eat and had come down to catch the tail end of the breakfast service.

"My mother says breakfast is the most important meal of the day." He sat down across from her without waiting for an invitation.

Leslie raised her eyebrows. She wasn't sure whether it was because he was being presumptuous or the fact that he actually had a mother. Curiosity won out. "You really have a mother?"

He grinned. "You know, I ought to be offended that you think I must have been dropped by Jack the Giant Killer, but yes, I have a mom. And a dad. And two older brothers."

She smiled. "Don't tell me you're the runt."

He laughed. "I won't because all the rest of the family is average height. They're not sure where I came from, and as my mom likes to say, she's not talking."

His mother sounded like she was as much a character as her son.

"You should smile more often," he said. "You look relaxed and happy when you do."

"I didn't know I looked like the Wicked Witch of the West," she said, dismayed. What did he mean she didn't look relaxed or happy? She was relaxed. She was happy. Well, as relaxed and happy as any person could be.

He made a face. "I said it wrong. I'm sorry. It's just that you always look . . . serious. No, businesslike. Until you laugh. That's so different, it takes a person by surprise. I think I'm digging a bigger hole for myself."

"Straight to China," she told him.

"What about your family?" he asked. "There, that's safe enough. Are they all tall too?"

She nodded while wondering whether to tell him about her marriage. Somehow that seemed far too intimate. She had to remember that Gerry's premonition really had no credence, and even though she liked Mike on some level, he'd already proven himself all wrong for her. Still, talking about her family wasn't a loss of control. In fact the sexual awareness was staying in the background at the moment. The last thing she needed was it popping to the fore, so mom and dad were an ideal topic. Nothing killed thoughts of sex faster than one's parents.

"My mom is tall, but my dad isn't, and neither is my younger brother. They're all accountants."

"You strayed far from the tree."

She chuckled. "Real far. Actually I hate number crunching, which was probably the only thing that kept me from becoming an accountant. And tax time. My parents have their own business. I used to feel as if my lips were glued shut during

March and April, from licking all those envelopes."

"My parents teach elementary and high school. I didn't stray at all from the tree, but I think I would have preferred having my lips glued shut for a couple of months to having both of them for teachers."

"You didn't."

He nodded. "Yes, both. My mother for fourth grade and my father for biology. We lived in a small town in Bucks County, so the schools were small too."

She envisioned him as a standout, especially in those formative teenage years when it must have been embarrassing to be the tallest kid *and* have one's dad for a teacher. The kids must have been cruel. . . .

She realized that by knowing more about him, she was becoming even more interested in him. That was a mistake. A big one. It aroused all kinds of gentler emotions in her, and the last thing she wanted was to soften to him. If her emotions softened, then her body wouldn't be far behind, and she'd find herself in a vacation fling yet. But lurking in the back of her mind were Gerry's words about finding a man on this trip. They were like a seduction, luring her onward with the first man *she'd* met. Foolish, very, very foolish. Well, it would all be over tomorrow when she left for Cornwall. Now was the time to get herself back in proper sensible order.

Simply looking at Mike, though, conjured up that vibrant awareness that threatened all her sensibilities. Darn, but he just looked really good with his blue eyes and square jaw. And he could be funny. Very funny.

Get hold of yourself! she mentally snapped.

Her breakfast arrived, and Leslie found herself tucking into it with more enthusiasm than the night before. She *was* hungry. Still, she said to Mike, "I think I'll take a nap after this. I really am wiped out."

He nodded.

She wished she believed it as much as he did. But the sooner she stopped seeing him, the better she could get back into her normal state of inner equilibrium.

Unfortunately that was sounding far too sane and sensible.

The next day Mike strolled along Bayswater Road, wanting and needing to clear his head. Leslie had come as a surprise to him. In fact she looked to be surprise after surprise. The kiss they had shared yesterday morning had stirred his blood so quick, he was still dazed from it. She was tall enough that he hadn't felt she would break in two when he held her, and that had been unexpectedly delightful. Their impromptu breakfast yesterday had only confirmed his attraction to her. If he was around her much more, he'd lose all sense of focus. Considering that he held a master belt in Tang Soo Do, that would be the ultimate shock. Twenty years of specialized karate training ought to ensure that a man knew how to keep his focus. Ought to. He was having trouble around her.

"Damn," he mumbled. She had him doing all kinds of things he normally didn't do—such as delaying his research on Jonson, even forgetting how to keep his brain on its proper course. Maybe she was right about him being absent-minded. His mind certainly seemed out to lunch ever since he'd met her.

Thinking of Leslie seemed to conjure her out of the thin air, because he saw her head, a head above most everyone else's in the noon-time crowd. Her hair was shining in the sun, hanging loose to her shoulders. Wonderful shoulders, he thought. Slender and yet held straight and proud. He liked that. In fact he liked it so much, he wanted to reach out and touch them, peel away the shirt she was wearing until he exposed the creamy flesh. It had to be creamy. He'd be very disappointed if it wasn't.

His brain belatedly reminded him there were more important matters at hand.

She'd slept the day and night away, he knew. He'd called her several times to check. When she'd finally answered her phone that morning, she'd told him she was still too tired to face breakfast. He'd wondered then if he was being obvious. The only thing that was obvious now was that Leslie had lied to him.

Could she be trying to put him off?

She just didn't know him well enough yet, he thought, stepping up his pace to follow her. They had met under odd circumstances, after all. There was no mutual acquaintance who could say, yes, Mike's a nice guy. He'd have to show her that.

Belatedly he realized that following her wasn't exactly a straight-and-narrow track to nice-guy land. He was relieved when she turned into a bank, and decided he had a traveler's check or two that needed cashing.

"Hi!" he said cheerfully when he got within her hearing.

She jerked in surprise, her mouth gaping for a second. "Hi."

He got in line behind her. "I see you've recovered from your all-nighter."

"Barely," she admitted.

"Sightseeing today? I could show you the—"

"I slept through my sightseeing day unfortunately." She made a face. "Damn, but that makes me mad. I only had one day for London."

"You can't see London in one day," he said, astonished at the notion.

She stared at him, then handed the clerk a check before turning back to him. "Of course you can't see London in a day. I didn't intend to see all of it. Just a quick tour on one of those sightseeing buses, then maybe the Tower and Buckingham Palace. You make your priorities of what you must see, then everything else is gravy."

"Oh." It was logical. Which figured. He'd always found it more fun just to drive down a country lane, or wander mapless along a city street, and find what was at the end of it, but refrained from saying so. She might not appreciate the advice. "So what are you doing now?"

"Getting money changed."

"No, I mean this afternoon."

"Getting my car. I should have gotten it this morning, but I'm running late." As if to emphasize her point, she yawned. "Sorry."

"Have you driven on the left side before?" he asked.

"No—" The clerk handed over her English money. She put it in her purse. "Well, goodbye."

"Wait for me," he said, slapping down a check.

"I can't. I'm already very late." She disappeared back out onto the sidewalk.

Mike practically growled at the clerk to hurry him, not caring if he was adding to the American-tourist reputation of being on the fast track to nowhere. As soon as he got his money, he was out the door, shoving the notes into his two jacket pockets as he flew after Leslie. He caught up with her a short block away.

"Hi again," he said cheerfully.

"Hi."

"If you haven't driven on the left side of the road before, it's pretty tricky—"

"I'm sure I'll get the hang of it. I've got to, actually, or else I don't get to Cornwall tonight."

"Cornwall! Who would go to Cornwall?"

"I would, for one thing."

"I mean," he said, realizing how he'd sounded, "why are you going to Cornwall?"

"I'm a tourist, remember."

He frowned. "I know you're a tourist, but that's not good thinking, driving by yourself—"

"It may not be good thinking, but I don't have a choice. We'll need a car in Cornwall to get around."

"We?"

She looked at him as if he had grown two heads. "Gerry and I. She's meeting me there."

"Oh." Relief washed over him. Then he frowned again. "But I thought you were going to Shropshire. That's northwest. Cornwall's southwest."

She snorted. "Yes, I know. But Shropshire isn't the only place we're going."

"Oh, you're doing your own tour." He nodded in agreement. She looked wonderful in her oxford shirt and denim skirt, the clothes emphasizing the long, graceful lines of her body. "Yes, of course. Why wouldn't you?"

But now he had a different dilemma. How could he let her drive the six hours to Cornwall by herself? He knew that once they separated, he would never meet up with her again. He didn't know enough about her life back home yet to find her there . . . and he didn't want to wait that long to see her again anyhow.

"Well, here's the car-rental offices." Mike woke up from his musings to find Leslie a few steps behind him, stopped in front of a white building with a faux Regency-period facade. "I won't hold you up any longer—"

"You're not." He took her arm, walking her inside the building, marveling at the willowiness of her limbs. Touching her set his blood pounding hard through his veins. Her light scent had his head spinning. Already he was recognizing and responding to her uniqueness.

He became aware that he was still holding her arm when she tried to step away from him. Reluctantly he dropped his hand.

"Thanks for bringing me inside—"

"No problem." He smiled and took a seat.

She stared at him, eyes wide. "What are you doing?"

"Sitting down."

"I see that. *Why* are you sitting down?"

"It's been my experience that people have a long wait in these places." He patted his pockets, remembered her former reaction to his pipe, and sighed instead.

She said quickly, "I appreciate it, but you don't have to wait with me."

She really did have beautiful eyes, Mike

thought. Dark hazel, fathomless, mysterious. A man could spend a lifetime staring into them and still never be quite sure what she was thinking. A voice penetrated his deliberations. "Mmmm?"

"*I said,*" she said loudly, "that you don't have to wait for me. You can go on with whatever you were doing."

"But I wasn't doing anything." He decided he would have to spend extra time in meditation. His focus was all screwed up.

"Then go and do anything," Leslie said, through clearly clenched teeth. "You're in London. Surely there are things *you* want to see."

"But I've seen London before. Once you've seen it, you've seen it."

"May I help you?" a woman asked, coming up behind Leslie.

Leslie whirled around. "I hope so. My travel agent reserved a car for me . . ."

Mike settled in to wait.

Leslie looked at the car with dismay.

It was a familiar American model on the outside, but the steering wheel was on the passenger side. She wondered if the gas and brake pedals were reversed too. She hoped not.

". . . and we provide you with maps," the woman said, finishing up her monologue on agency provisions.

"Take the train," Mike advised, wise for once in their short acquaintance.

Leslie swallowed and gave the only answer she could. "Can I buy that extra optional insurance you talked about?"

She would need it, she thought. It was another couple of minutes before the last of the paperwork was signed, then Leslie slipped behind the wheel of the car. The only saving grace was that the pedals *were* in the right places.

The car started with little trouble. She gingerly put it in reverse. The rental agent and Mike looked on—from a safe distance—she smiling with encouragement and he frowning with doubt. Leslie eased on the gas. The car shot backward and she turned the wheel . . . the wrong way. She slammed on the brakes, just missing another car. Its side-view mirror, on a rubber base, was bent backward to the snapping point.

Her hands shaking, she wondered how she was supposed to get back to the hotel, let alone across the breadth of England. Overwhelmed, she swallowed back a lump of despair at being abandoned in a foreign country. Normally she and Gerry would be laughing at this point, but now she wanted to kill her friend. Former friend. This was the worst.

The car door opened. Mike poked his head in. "Get out and get in the other side. I'll drive you to the hotel."

"No." She smiled—or tried to. Her upper lip

felt stuck to her two front teeth. "Thanks for the offer, really, but I can do this. I have to." She nudged him out of the way and shut the door. Checking for traffic, she pushed up the turn signal stalk . . . and the wipers slashed back and forth over the windshield.

Leslie turned off the car. She rolled down the window and held the keys out to Mike.

"Thank you," she whispered, eternally grateful—and hopeful that if she watched someone else driving, she'd get the hang of it. She got out and went back into the building to sign him up on the policy. They were back in the car a few minutes later, she safely in the passenger seat.

Mike settled into the driver's seat, pushing it back as far as it would go. He still looked as if he could steer with his knees. He started the car efficiently and, with a couple of turns of the wheel, got the vehicle out of its current predicament and onto the busy Bayswater Road. He drove like a pro, having no problem with being on the opposite side of the road.

She watched his hands as they gripped the wheel. His fingers were long and strong-looking—certainly very competent. His profile was strong, too, she thought. She liked the way his shock of straight hair hung on his forehead, and the way it curled just at the collar of his shirt. Her fingers itched to brush it out of the way. His glasses hardly detracted from his looks. In fact they gave him an intense air. She had a disconcerting feeling that beyond the vague "two steps behind the world" exterior was a sharp brain that missed nothing.

Too bad they were so incompatible. She would have liked him a lot if he was in sync with her better. And if they had met at home, under normal circumstances. . . .

She could turn this into normal circumstances if she tried. She could already see the ending of any relationship that might start here.

"You drive on the right on the left side," he said, turning the wheel clockwise instead of counterclockwise to give space between the cars parked along the curb.

Leslie blinked. "What?"

"You're driving on the right in the car, so you must drive on the left on the road."

"I'll have an accident within a minute," she said, having her own premonitions for once. More like nightmares.

"London streets are hardly the place to learn to drive."

"No kidding."

"I wasn't, actually. What kind of car do you drive back home?"

"A nice, familiar Ford," she replied.

"Me too. I've got a silver Crown Victoria."

She laughed. "I've got a gray one."

At the same time they said, "Leg room."

She could chalk up one thing in common. They had the same car for the same reason.

Funny, she thought. She would have pictured him as more the flower-power Volkswagen van type.

"Here we are." He swung the car into a quick right-hand turn that disturbingly crossed the traffic lanes, then pulled into the hotel's parking lot.

Leslie leaned back against the headrest. Sensibility told her she was doomed if she tried to drive to Cornwall alone. Granted, she and Gerry would have been just as doomed, but somehow everything seemed easier to take with a friend.

"How about if I drive you to Cornwall?"

She shot upright, staring at Mike. "You'd drive me to Cornwall?"

"You'll never get out of London without getting killed, let alone survive the M roads. That's England's highway system. I can drive you down, then take a train back. And as we go, you can get in some practice along the country roads, through Wiltshire and Devon."

The invitation was astonishing. Leslie couldn't believe anyone would do it on the spur of the moment. How could he? And why would he? It didn't make any sense.

The invitation had a more dangerous side too. Being enclosed in a small space with him would only heighten her sensual awareness of him. She was already having a lot of trouble with that as it was.

She couldn't, she thought. She hardly knew him. He hardly knew her. Tempting as the invitation was, she couldn't. "Why would you do this?"

"Because I hate to see a fellow American get killed on foreign highways. We do that enough at home. Besides, it gives us a bad reputation as tourists."

"But you have things to do, surely."

"They can wait a little . . . and don't call me Shirley." He grinned. "I saw that movie too."

So had she, and she hadn't cared for it. That just showed again how incompatible they were. "Although I appreciate your offer, I can't let you. You have your sabbatical—"

"Leslie, you don't have a choice. Just ask your common sense that. Cambridge and Jonson can wait a few days."

She was afraid to allow him to drive, she thought. She knew what answer her common sense would give, and she was in no mood to hear it. But a little piece of it got through anyway, telling her that he was absolutely right and she was being a fool not to recognize that. If she had a chance to adjust on the easier roads, she'd be fine for driving during the rest of the trip.

But with how she was already responding to him, more time spent with him could lead to more intimacy. She began a rejection again, one kind of common sense winning out over the other. "I couldn't ask you to do that—"

"I'm not asking you to ask me. I'm telling you, for your own sake, I'm coming with you." He smiled. "It won't be so bad, I promise. And if

I do anything annoying, you can dump me right on the spot. Okay?"

"Okay." Although she still sounded reluctant, she was privately relieved. Very relieved. They'd get the car down there, and that was the important thing.

At least that's what she tried to tell herself.

THREE

"Now, just remember to keep to the left side of the road, especially when you turn corners."

Mike leaned over the console, trying not to rub his shoulder against Leslie's while instructing her. They had gotten off the main highway outside of Devises in Wiltshire, to give her a first driving lesson on the Salisbury Plain. The plain spread out around them, the little roadway a black ribbon that curled over and around lonely, windswept downs. A house or a copse of trees dotted the barrenness here and there, barely breaking the horizon of green grasses.

"This place must be bleak in the winter," he commented, glancing out the windshield. He'd never been here in the winter. . . .

"Forget that," Leslie said. "Since I'm on the other side of the car, do I have to turn the wheel opposite of the way I want to go? Please say no."

He sighed. She was so damned practical. "No."

She gave him an apologetic look. "I know I'm a pain in the tush. You didn't have to come along."

He just stared back at her, saying nothing. She fiddled with turn-signal and windshield-wiper stalks, as if trying to get them sorted out in her mind.

Mike smiled. The "schoolteacher stare" worked every time. Now they could get back to the lesson. Or try to.

It wasn't easy with the way her scent teased at his senses. He was aware of the curve of her breast just next to his arm. If he leaned a little closer . . .

She sat back suddenly, her shoulder rubbing his. He straightened, almost jumping out of the way of their touch.

"What did I do wrong?" she asked, edging away from him as if contact with him had burned her. He hoped it did, in a way.

"Nothing." He sighed again. She was all business and common sense—except when she kissed. Then she was a passionate woman, waiting to get out. Sitting next to her thus far on the trip had been an exercise in torture. He wanted to reach out . . . kiss her again . . . touch her . . .

He shook his head, thinking he was thinking in very wrong patterns. Leslie's safety should be the number-one priority, getting to know her better the second, and physical attraction the third.

If things continued like this, the physical attraction would be *all* priority, and they'd probably get killed before they could get to know each other better. He'd have to get a grip, or they could be in really serious trouble—or on the side of the road making love. Maybe making love was premature, he thought as images of her naked and wanton in his arms flashed through his brain. But they'd be making something, for damn sure.

Leslie edged out onto the road, getting his attention back into proper perspective. The car slowly gathered speed until they were doing twenty-five—miles, not kilometers, per hour. They putted along for about ten minutes at the same speed. She was doing fine on the lonely little road, but Mike figured at this rate they'd make Cornwall in about two days.

"You're doing great," he said out loud.

"It's not so bad," she commented, then added, "here."

Out of nowhere a horn blared from behind, as if to make a liar of her. Leslie immediately cut the wheel to the right, the way an American driver would go to get off the road—and nearly put them into the path of the passing car. Mike grabbed the wheel and swung it to the left, swerving them onto the verge. The other driver glared as he passed, mouthing words that didn't need to be heard to know their meaning.

He'd wanted to be on the side of the road with her, Mike thought ruefully. He'd have to be careful what he wished for in the future.

"Out your ear!" Leslie said to the back of the other car as it sped down the road. "Can't you see I'm learning?"

Mike started laughing. For someone so seemingly predictable, she could be surprising.

She grinned wryly and shrugged. "I know, I know. I forgot the side of the road was on the left. But it was almost like he was trying to run me off the road."

"Shall we try again?" he asked, ignoring her last comment. A person would have to be paranoid to think the incident had been deliberate.

"If we don't," she said, "we'll never get to Cornwall, and you'll never get back to London."

He wondered how he could tell her he wasn't going back to London without her thinking him some kind of nut or masher or worse. It would be tricky. It could be impossible.

That was a bridge he'd cross when he came to it, for he wasn't going back just yet. Not until he knew Leslie a whole lot better. If a person didn't follow a crazy impulse once in a while, great things could be missed.

They drove along without mishap, Leslie getting more confident as they did. A car or two passed them, but she didn't panic. The countryside became more wild, more lonely, and more lovely under the bright summer sun—and the woman next to him more sexy by the moment.

Mike was moved to quote Robert Browning. " 'If you get simple beauty and naught else, you get about the best thing God invents.' "

The car screeched to a halt, stalling out as they crested a hill, and Leslie exclaimed, "Look at that! Look at that!"

Mike looked at the famous circle of stones in the distance. "Stonehenge, yes." He glanced back to her and delighted in her expression of awe and astonishment. He had the urge to kiss her and astonish her more, but reality intruded. "Now that we've admired it, get moving before we get walloped from behind."

"Oh!" She started the engine again and pressed down on the gas. The car shot forward. She fought the wheel for a second, then righted it onto the proper side of the road.

"I wish we could see it," she said wistfully.

"We can stop and take the tour of the stones," he said. He'd like nothing better than the two of them strolling hand in hand around the ancient stones, feeling the subtle power that emanated from them. He knew it was primitive, almost sensual, and he wanted her to experience it with him.

"No," she said, shaking her head. "We've got to get to Cornwall. Gerry will be waiting."

And waiting and waiting, Mike thought as they proceeded carefully along the roadway. Stonehenge meant they were only about halfway to the Cornish town of Falmouth, where Leslie was staying.

Traffic got heavier around the historic site. Mike pointed out the barrows on the hills around the stones. The burial mounds of great Celtic chieftains were now grassy humps in the earth.

Fascinating, he thought, wondering who they had been and how they had lived. "Look over there—"

"I can't look now!" Leslie said as a car suddenly cut in front of her. Her knuckles were white where she gripped the steering wheel.

Mike shook his head in dismay. They just didn't meet on the same level, he thought. It wasn't that her job was so different from his or that they didn't know each other that well yet. In some basic way they were opposite. That made her exasperating . . . and fascinating.

He watched her long legs ease against each other as she stepped on brake and gas pedals. Slow side-to-side movements that sent his head spinning. He wanted to feel those legs easing against his own. Whatever was not connecting when they spoke didn't matter when he considered the physical attraction.

They traveled south out of the plain, a slightly longer route, Mike knew, but with lots of one-lane roads that allowed Leslie to get really comfortable driving.

He enjoyed playing navigator, especially when he was able to take them past several other ancient monuments. Leslie was relaxing enough to actually take a look at one or two of them. He loved finding new things, viewing new things, sharing knowledge.

"Here's the Cerne Giant," he said as the road curved around a huge figure cut into the downs. The giant was outlined in the white chalk that lay just under the turf.

Leslie seemed to start. At least the car jerked a little when she looked.

"See his war club?" Mike went on. "He's a Celtic god of the hunt. And with his engorged genitalia, he's also the god of fertility."

Leslie made a funny choking noise. Mike ignored it as he continued his lecture.

"An abbey actually used to sit at the foot of the figure. I'm surprised they didn't wipe it out hundreds of years ago as pornography. He's pretty blatant. I understand the villagers come out and keep the chalk clear about every decade or so, so that the outline stays distinctive. The Celts were a practical people two thousand years ago, combining sustenance and propagation together in one big lump of a god. As a time management person you'll appreciate that—"

"No doubt," Leslie said, speeding up to pass the huge figure.

"What's the hurry?" Mike asked, looking back. "We could stop for a minute or two and look."

"No, no, we have to move on—"

He turned to her, amazed at her determination. "Leslie, you have passed by every single historic site between here and London. You really wanted to stop at Stonehenge, I could tell. Now, come on. Here's a great bit of ancient history. We need a stretch anyway, and what's a few minutes in the scheme of things?"

"You'd be amazed what a few minutes in the scheme of things can save. Besides, I'm not stopping *here.*"

"Are you chicken?" he asked, when it occurred to him she might actually be embarrassed. Not Leslie, he thought. But if she was, he wasn't about to let her get away with it. This was history, not sex, but if she was beginning to think in those terms, he certainly wanted to further them.

"No, I'm not chicken," she replied in a testy tone. To his satisfaction she did slow down and direct the car off the road, coming to a stop.

Mike grinned as he scrambled out of the front seat.

Leslie got out of the driver's side more reluctantly. Mike came around the car and took her arm. "He won't bite."

She made a face. "Are you sure about that?"

A shepherd came over the crest of the hill, driving a small group of sheep in front of him. They were herded right across the chest of the giant. Nothing could have said "bucolic innocence" better than such an obvious, everyday occurrence.

Mike smiled, waving to the shepherd. "Look at that. The giant's harmless, trust me. I'm the one you have to worry about on that score."

She muttered something that he didn't catch. He admitted he didn't want to. He'd have to be careful of flirting too much, since she'd entrusted herself to him, a relative stranger. Still, he couldn't resist. If she ever truly let go of all that logic and relaxed . . . He'd love to see that.

As they walked up the hill, closer to the enormous figure, he found his attention focusing on her body just bare inches away from his. Her skin where his hand touched her above her elbow was warm and smooth, like marble come to life. It would be so easy to turn her to him, kiss her again. He set the thought aside, reminding himself of the control he needed to exert.

He tried conversation to take his mind off sex. "The figure looks simplistic, doesn't it? But do you see the definition of his ribs and the muscular curve of his thighs? Impressive detail."

"I didn't notice."

"Then allow me to help you. Look at that butt. Hubba, hubba."

Leslie burst into laughter.

Mike grinned, liking the sound of it. The last thing he'd expected from her was Victorian prudery. Knowing how she kissed, that only added to the intrigue of this fascinating, contradictory woman.

As they stood at the edge of the outline, Leslie

bent down and touched the exposed white earth. "It *is* like chalk, isn't it?"

"That's why they call it that. By the way, they say if you touch the figure, you'll cure all your infertility problems."

She immediately stood up, brusquely brushing her hands off. "Not when you're single, thank you very much."

"Don't you want children?" he asked.

"Yes, but I'm not crazy about the idea of single motherhood. At least for me. My biological clock may be ticking away, but the alarm hasn't gone off yet."

"I'm not interested in single fatherhood, either," he admitted.

"There's something to the idea of having someone suffer through parenthood with you, isn't there?" she said, smiling at him. "My brother and I fought all the time and drove my parents crazy, so I know."

"In my house it was my two older brothers. They fought over everything." Mike grinned. "I was the angel."

Leslie made a rude noise, then said, "Well, that's enough gratuitous sex and violence from giants and siblings. Let's get going."

"He could be a Chippendale dancer," Mike said, not able to resist one last shot as they walked back down the hill.

She glanced over at him. "I'm surprised you know what they are."

"Of course I know what they are," he said, chuckling. "Guys with great bodies who put the rest of us to shame. Women drool over them. I've seen pictures. Temple University is hardly an ivory tower. Have you ever drooled over any? Chippendale dancers, I mean."

"I plead the Fifth," she answered primly.

He roared with laughter.

"Okay, so I've been dragged to a male dancing show by Gerry a time or two." She shrugged. "No big deal. Besides, you men have had your *Playboys* for years."

"I plead the Fifth," he said, in as prim a tone as she had used.

She giggled. She actually giggled. He had a feeling she didn't get silly very often. It wouldn't be logical. He'd have to work on that.

But thanks to the Cerne Giant, she was thinking in the right direction. It was nice to know the magic still worked in the twentieth century.

"I made it!" Leslie exclaimed with relief as she turned the car into the drive of the Palisades Hotel and parked in front of the steps. Lanterns on either side of the double doors at the top of the short stairs had a welcoming twinkle.

"You did good," Mike complimented her. "Although I had to drive over the Tamar River Bridge—"

"I certainly wasn't about to!" she declared. It

had been one hellish span. But she knew he was teasing her, because he had suggested he drive the bridge in the first place. Actually a sensible decision on his part. In fact he'd been almost sensible throughout the whole trip.

That kind of thinking was dangerous, she told herself, for she was getting to know him more and more and liking him more and more. And sitting in a car with him for hours had been the torture she'd feared.

Lord, but he filled a space. He couldn't be ignored through his sheer size. He was turned toward her now, smiling at her, causing her heart to flip over, making her want to reach out and thread her fingers through his hair. Just to feel the way the silky strands would tickle her palms. She wanted to touch his cheek, run her finger over his jaw, pull him to her for a second kiss. One that would put the first one in the shade.

She was getting it bad, she thought. What she needed was space and plenty of it.

She got out of the car and stretched. Every bone and muscle in her body ached, but she could feel her awareness dissipating.

Mike got out from the passenger side. Stumbled out was more like it. He leaned on the hood of the car, groaning as he tried to work the kinks out of his back.

"I'm sorry," she said, feeling for him. "I wish we could have stopped more often."

"No, it's okay," he said, raising his head. "I get like this just going to the supermarket."

"Liar."

"Right. I'd kill for a bed. Anything flat."

She smiled, then frowned. "But you have to catch a train back—"

"Leslie, there are no trains at this hour," he interrupted in a voice that would break stone. "I need a room and a bed and no argument from you."

"I'm sane and sensible," she said. "Why would I argue?"

"I have no idea, but I could feel you leading up to one."

Okay, she thought, so maybe she was about to suggest he wait at the station for the next train because she hadn't been thinking properly. Logistics dictated that there was no train until morning. But with him staying the night, she didn't know how she would get her confused thoughts back in line. "Thank you, Mike, for helping me out like this. I don't know what I would have done without you."

"Had an accident." He smiled. "I'm glad I could be of assistance."

"Do you help strangers out like this all the time?" He did do things differently from the rest of the world. It was possible he didn't blink twice at this stuff.

"Only for tall, willowy brunettes."

She swallowed. That settled that.

He laughed. "Relax. Tempting as you are, right now I couldn't ravage a teddy bear."

"I think I'll just go register." If she let the sexy teasing continue, she could be in big trouble.

They took her and Gerry's bags out of the trunk, and they walked up the steps. The doors were locked. Mike looked along the lintel, then rang a bell. Leslie sighed in relief that he knew what to do. She'd had a moment of panic that the hotel had locked them out. Next time it was definitely Hiltons all the way.

The lights came on, and a yawning woman in her fifties, wearing a wildly patterned robe, let them in.

"My poor dears, it's so late!" she exclaimed as she ushered them into the hall. Leslie recognized the voice as that of the owner, Mrs. Drago, whom she'd spoken with on the telephone before.

"I'm sorry," she began, but Mrs. Drago cut her off.

"Nonsense! Nothing to be sorry about. Let's get you registered. Oh, you *are* the Americans who called earlier, right?"

"Yes."

She chuckled. "This is later than even you had thought."

"Has Gerry O'Hanlon arrived?" Leslie asked as she filled out the registration card.

"Isn't that Gerry O'Hanlon?" Mrs. Drago asked, pointing to Mike, who was bringing in the bags.

"No. Oh, no!" Leslie said quickly. She wondered if everyone would mistake them for lovers. She hated explaining they weren't. It was embarrassing. Still, a primitive sensation went through her at the thought, and she wondered if she hated it only because it wasn't true. That giant was still pretty damn effective after all these centuries. "He's Mike Smith. He helped me get my rental car down here." She asked unhappily, "Then Gerry hasn't arrived?"

"No. I have no other Americans here. He is American, this Gerry?"

"She."

"No, she didn't arrive today either. I'm sorry, dear." Mrs. Drago looked sympathetic.

Leslie ground her teeth together. Damn her! Damn her! Gerry was supposed to be here by now.

"I'll need a room," Mike said, straightening to his full height. It was a little like watching a polar bear rising up on its hind legs. One minute he looked benign, even cute, and in the next he looked absolutely menacing.

Mrs. Drago blinked. "My, you are a tall one."

"He was taking an evening train back to London, but it's too late. Do you have a room for him?"

"Let me see."

Mrs. Drago began thumbing through her cards. Leslie waited in dread, wondering if it would be like a thirties comedy and they would be stuck sharing. She'd sleep in the car first, because she had the awful feeling that once she was in the same room with him, she'd turn into Zelda, the desperate man-eater from the old "Dobie Gillis" television show.

"I have a little single," the woman said finally.

Leslie breathed a sigh of relief.

"*Little* single?" Mike's expression was apprehensive.

Leslie giggled. He really could be funny at times.

"Just a bed and a bath stand, really. I'm afraid that's all I've got at the moment."

"He'll take it," Leslie said.

"I will?" Mike blinked owlishly behind his glasses.

She smiled sweetly at him. "It's either that or the car again."

"I'll take it," he said.

Mrs. Drago showed them to their rooms, chattering away about the lovely swimming pool the hotel had. It was the de-luxe point of attraction evidently. They dropped her off first. When Leslie finally shut the door, she sank back against the polished wood.

It wasn't fair, she thought. Gerry was off having a wonderful time with the maybe-future Mr. O'Hanlon, and she was stuck doing their vacation alone. Somehow it sounded selfish, but she wasn't sure who was the guilty party. She ought to be glad she'd made it down to Cornwall in one piece.

"Gerry *will* show up," she willed out loud, facing her unpacking.

She was only ten minutes into the job, when someone knocked on her door.

"Who is it?" she asked.

"Mike."

For a moment she wondered if she should open it or not. The last time he had been in a hotel room with her, sparks had flown. And with her awareness heightened by hours and hours in the car with him, she was ready to set those sparks to a flame. She didn't need more sparks, but she couldn't leave him out there. *Just be sensible and remember you aren't here for a vacation fling or to fulfill one of Gerry's cockeyed premonitions*, she told herself firmly.

She opened the door.

"Hi." Mike stared over her head at the two double beds, the big dresser, and the wardrobe, a wistful expression on his face. "I have hangers on a peg, a washstand, the bathroom's down the hall, and the bed's at least a foot too short."

"Every bed must be a foot too short for you," she said.

He gazed down at her. "Your bed looks bigger . . . and you have an extra one."

"Don't even think it," she warned, although her senses stirred traitorously at the thought. More than stirred, they darn near whipped themselves into a frenzy.

"I can dream. And I would be a gentleman.

Okay, okay." He sighed. "You're all right in here, then?"

"I'm fine. Can I go to sleep now?"

"I suppose. Dream of me in my agony."

He leaned forward and kissed her on the mouth. An easy kiss, a kiss of promise. Then he left. And she did dream of him.

The agony was sheer pleasure.

"You're what!"

Mike tried to smile, but Leslie's shocked face didn't give him a good feeling. He wished he'd gotten a better night's sleep. Not only was the bed too short, it was too lumpy. Goldilocks had gotten a better deal at the bear hotel. He repeated, "I'm staying for a couple of days. I haven't been to Cornwall in ages. The pasties . . . the clotted cream . . . the lonely cliffs. It inspires one to commune with nature—"

"What about your hotel in London? What about your sabbatical? They're waiting for you in Cambridge, remember?"

He *would* have to have told her about that. "I don't feel right leaving you here either. I'll just wait for your friend to show—"

"I'm perfectly capable of staying here by myself." She stared at him, unmindful of the people seated around them at breakfast. She hadn't raised her voice, but it had to be obvious she was unhappy with him. "Mike, I appreciate all you've done for me. I would have been lost trying to get down here on my own, and I can't thank you enough. But you *can't* stay—"

"Why not?" he asked, taking his turn to interrupt. The way she emphasized the word *can't* gave him hope. He glanced around to see if anyone was taking an inordinate interest in their discussion. No one was. "You still may have trouble with the car, you know. Cornwall's loaded with narrow, steep roads. Not the best driving."

"I can manage."

"Right."

This wasn't going too badly, he thought. She was focused on the what, not the why. He wanted to take this slowly, after all. As long as she didn't worry about why he wanted to stay, he might be okay. Logical people liked puzzles, and Lord knows his staying was a puzzler for her. If she got started . . .

"Why *are* you staying?" she asked, raising her eyebrows.

She had started. Mike groaned inwardly.

"I told you. I haven't been in Cornwall for years. I love the food and the atmosphere. I have time to kill, and you still may need some help."

"You've been in England for a while, so why didn't you come down earlier if you love it here that much? Sabbatical leaves may be fluid, but hardly spur-of-the-moment. None of that stands up, Mike."

He stared at her for one long moment, his

brain scrambling for innocent answers. He couldn't leave. Every bone in his body objected fiercely to even the notion of being away from Leslie. He couldn't understand the impulsive need himself, let alone explain it to her. Finally he said the only thing that he could think of.

"I want to sleep with you."

Leslie's hands banged down on the table. Her fingers hit the edge of her coffee cup. It seemed to take a little hop, then tilted. The liquid hovered for one instant, steaming and black, before shooting out across the white tablecloth. People stared. Leslie stared. Mike groaned again.

"Oh, dear! Oh, dear!" Mrs. Drago sputtered, hustling over to the table. She whisked the cloth out from under the china and silverware, mopping as she went.

"I'm sorry," Mike said, knowing it was his fault.

As soon as Mrs. Drago left, Leslie leaned forward, her eyes wide with emotion. She whispered, "*What* did you say?"

Mike ground his teeth together, then whispered back, "I want to sleep with you. What's so difficult about that? I'm a man. You're a woman who's not eye-to-eye with my belly button for once."

"You want to sleep with me because I'm taller than the average babe?"

"No. Yes." He rubbed his forehead against the headache that threatened. She made it sound so . . . tawdry. How the hell had he gotten into this mess? "You're an attractive woman, Leslie. Why wouldn't any man?"

She burst into laughter. Mike could feel the heat suffusing his face.

"I'm not a masher," he said in his own defense.

She laughed even more. He noticed everyone else grinning and nodding. He doubted they had heard the actual discussion, but were relieved that the arguing couple at Table 4 had now made up.

"Well, it's lovely to see people start the day so cheerful," Mrs. Drago said, bustling up with a new tablecloth.

"I agree," Leslie got out before dissolving into chuckles again.

Once the table was reset and Mrs. Drago on her way to another breakfast calamity, Mike ground out, "Dammit, Leslie. Anyone ever tell you that you can deflate a man's ego in two seconds flat?"

"Only you would come across a country in the hopes of a good time."

"What do you mean, only me?" he asked, frowning.

"Only an absentminded professor would follow some woman he just met across England rather than pick up a woman on the local London streetcorner."

"You make me sound like a stalker! *I* told you to forget the car and take the train, remember? If you had, you wouldn't have needed me to drive. *You* brought me down here. You're the one who didn't say no."

Suddenly her amusement turned cool. "I'm not interested in being anyone's sabbatical fling, and especially just because I'm the right height—!"

"There's a telephone call for you, miss."

Mike didn't think he was ever more grateful for an interruption than he was at that moment. Leslie was working herself up into a real tear.

She got up to take the call, and he followed her out to the front desk and the only telephone, just like any self-respecting, absentminded professor would.

"Hello? Gerry?"

Leslie's frown deepened. Her mouth firmed into a grim line as her friend talked continuously for five minutes. Mike couldn't hear the words as he studied the wallpaper, but he could hear the frantic pleading in the voice.

"I don't believe this," Leslie said finally. "You've gone around the bend, Gerry. How can you say you love this man? You just met him three days ago."

Gerry wasn't coming. Mike tried not to grin.

The conversation went on a bit longer, just as it had the last time. Mike felt as if the pieces were coming into place for him, even as they were coming unglued for Leslie. He truly did feel bad for her, though. She'd spent a lot of money to come here, and now she was having a lousy time. He wished he could show her England as it truly should be seen—in the castles, in the cathedrals, in the country pubs. She would enjoy it, he was sure. Maybe he could give her a little of that. Maybe he could also fix the mess he'd just made of trying to tell her how he felt. He had made it sound as if his interest in her was only sexual and was based on only one factor. Height. No wonder she thought he was a nut.

Leslie dropped the receiver onto its cradle, a gesture oddly more ominous than slamming it back into place.

"Gerry not coming?" he asked.

"No."

That she didn't even snap at him was a measure of her unhappiness.

"Some friend," he ventured, realizing this was *not* the moment to broach an apology and explanation.

"I think she's gone insane from jet lag or something. This isn't like her at all."

"She and I seem to have the same problem," he mused, trying to lighten the mood for Leslie. "But I'm here—"

She snorted in disgust. "Mike, if that's your idea of perspective and sympathy, go take a cold shower."

"I can't. No bathroom, remember?" He let out his breath. "Look, this isn't fair to you at all. But I *am* here, and I will be a gentleman if that's what you want. Just a companion and, as a bonus, I actually know the area. It won't be any fun for you by yourself. At least get your money's worth while you're here, Leslie."

"Thanks, but no thanks," she replied, just as he'd expected. "I'll manage."

She went up to her room, skipping the rest of breakfast. Mike's stomach growled a protest, not allowing him to do the same. He didn't have much of a room anyway.

He went back into the dining room and took his seat, signaling to Mrs. Drago.

"My friend isn't feeling well just now," he told her, "but could someone take up a pot of coffee and maybe some pastries or rolls for her? She needs to eat something."

"Of course." Mrs. Drago grinned broadly, approving of his request.

"I'll have the kippers and eggs. Afterward can we find me a better room? One with a bed that would fit me?"

Mrs. Drago chuckled. "I think I can do you something, lovey."

Mike grinned. He would fix things with Leslie. He was here to stay.

FOUR

"I noticed you walked down from the hotel."

Leslie watched as Mike pulled out a chair at her sidewalk-café table and sat down. She hadn't seen him since Gerry's phone call a few hours earlier, and she hadn't wanted to—for several reasons.

She was only the right height, for goodness' sake. *Only* the right height. Here she was attracted to him in so many ways. She liked him more and more, despite their clear incompatibility. And he only liked her for her height. Well, it was a first. It left her amused and frustrated and insulted all at the same time.

Yet she had found herself actually daydreaming about him when she'd been in her room after the disappointment with Gerry. She had lain on her bed and without warning her mind's eye had conjured a vision of them wild with passion, almost clawing at each other, their mouths clinging, her legs wrapping around his hips. . . .

She shivered. It had been so vivid, so clear in that one moment. Like a premonition of what was to come.

"Penny for your thoughts," he said, grinning at her.

She flushed. She could feel that damnable telling heat on her face. He couldn't know what she was feeling. He couldn't.

"Mike, I thought you would have gone to Cambridge by now," she said finally, trying to cover her confusion in an emotionally defensive move.

"I will eventually, don't worry." He stopped a waitress and asked for scones, clotted cream, and tea, exactly what she was in the middle of eating. He turned back to her. "I didn't explain things well earlier. I like you for more than your height, you know. That might be the first thing I noticed about you, but the list keeps growing, Leslie Kloslosky."

"It does?" she couldn't help asking, flattered by his forthright approach—flattered that there was more to his attraction than two giraffes spotting each other over the treetops. Suddenly she was feeling better.

He smiled at her. "Definitely. I like talking to you, for one thing. I like showing you things—like the Cerne Giant."

She blushed again.

He chuckled. "You liked him. Admit it."

"He was . . . interesting. Can we talk about something else?"

"Of course, although you had your chance at Stonehenge for a more Platonic bit of history." He cleared his throat and said, "Beautiful day, isn't it? What have you been up to?"

"Not much. I went up to Pendennis Castle. It isn't much of a castle."

"Naturally it isn't much of a castle because it isn't a castle at all. It was a fortification built by Henry the Eighth, along with its twin just across the bay. They were a first defense against the threat of the Spanish. Did you notice the staircase going down to the cellar and how narrow it was compared with the ones going up to the top? That's because the servants lived downstairs and the generals lived upstairs. Fascinating that you can see how their class structure is reflected in even small things like steps."

"Fascinating," she said, watching the way his mouth moved. He really did have a beautiful mouth—firm, mobile lips that twitched slightly in a permanent smile. Nice white teeth too. This had to be unhealthy, sizing up a man's teeth, she thought. She decided she had completely lost her mind.

"Did you like the video of the battle scene?"

"I didn't see a video."

"You didn't see the video!" he exclaimed indignantly.

She shrugged. "All I saw was that empty first floor. It didn't seem like much, so I left."

"But you missed everything. Leslie, you have got to explore a place to get its flavor, to find the little things in life. You probably missed the deathbed-display upstairs too."

She had, but she did see a dimple that winked in and out of his cheek when he talked. That was fascinating too. Really, she thought, he was good-looking. Unfortunately a pretty face wasn't what counted in a relationship.

That she was even thinking of him in terms of a relationship was terrifying. This man was all wrong for her at the best of times, and very wrong right now because they were really like ships passing in the night. Answering any mating call of the foghorn wasn't sensible. Thinking of him as some kind of predestined mate was absolutely insane.

"How do you know so much about this?" she asked, to get her mind on a less confusing topic.

"I've been around." He said it like Humphrey Bogart in *The Maltese Falcon*, with mystery and promise. "I've been up and down the peninsula several times, including taking in Pendennis Castle. Once, over a Christmas, I even rented a seventeenth-century cottage near Land's End from the National Heritage."

"That must have been wonderful," she said,

now fascinated with the way his hair fell across his forehead. Like a boy's almost. "Almost" was the key. No boy could cause her hormone levels to elevate, let alone send them as high as this man did. But when he got enthusiastic, he had a certain cockeyed, whimsical charm.

His snack arrived. He raved to the waitress, who grinned flirtatiously at him before she went away again. Then he slathered his scone with the clotted cream until it looked like a strawberry shortcake without the strawberries, took a bite, and followed it with a sip of tea. He did it with much appreciative sighing. Leslie giggled at him. She couldn't help it. The absentminded professor definitely had one focus, and that was food.

His stomach clearly satisfied, he said, "Actually that Christmas was pretty bad. Darlene and I fought all the time."

"Darlene?" A sinking feeling started in Leslie's stomach. He had a Darlene? Who and what was she?

He nodded. "My wife."

Wife. Leslie cursed under her breath, all the physical attraction freezing with that one word. What was scarier was that it didn't die with that one word. And it should have. It definitely should have.

"Ex-wife actually. We've been divorced for several years."

Relief, far too much of it, shot through her. She shouldn't want to know more about him, though, she reminded herself. Knowing more created intimacy. And mental and emotional intimacy led to physical intimacy. She had to be more vigilant.

Unfortunately she was more curious than vigilant.

He stared at her. "I never did ask you . . . I mean, I made an assumption that you aren't married because you're traveling with a girlfriend, but are you? Married? Attached?"

She hesitated, wondering if she could get away with a lie. Maybe if he thought she was involved with someone, he'd go away. She doubted she could manage it. She had never been a good liar. "No. I'm divorced like you."

"Why?"

"Why what?"

"Why did you get a divorce?" He took a sip of his tea, looking not the least impertinent for asking.

Leslie hesitated again. This was personal, after all. But again, maybe if he knew the truth, he'd go away. "I was too dull."

He was taking another sip as she spoke, and his jaw dropped, tea spilling out of his mouth. Quickly he grabbed up his napkin and blotted his chin, managing to catch most of the liquid before it hit his shirtfront. "What? You're not serious."

She shrugged. "My husband said I was too dull."

"I guess he never went driving with you." Mike grinned. "What a horse's ass."

"I married the horse's ass," she said, feeling defensive because she had made a sane and sensible decision at the time.

"So you made a mistake. Everyone does."

She hated making mistakes, that was the problem. And no one was supposed to make a mistake about true love. In her case true love had lasted about a year and a half before she knew something was wrong in her marriage. Somehow "sane and sensible" combined with "true love" had failed.

"Okay, so what went wrong with your marriage?" she asked.

"I was too tall."

She gaped at him. "You're kidding."

"No."

"You *are* kidding. Being too tall is ridiculous!"

He shook his head. "No, it isn't. Darlene was five foot three, and that was in heels. We couldn't dance because she wound up with her head in a delicate place on my body, and sex was an exercise in restraint. I think she got tired of having to stand on a chair every time we kissed. Her new husband is five foot six, and she's happy as a clam. Now do you understand why I latched on to you?"

"Oh, yes," she muttered, disgusted. "I won't be dancing in your . . . ahem . . . and I probably won't break in bed. Gee, thanks, but no thanks."

He smiled, a glint of arousal in his eyes. "No, you won't break in bed, Leslie. However, I think the *bed* may break."

Her instant vision was back, this time so vivid, she could taste his mouth on hers, feel his lips on her breasts, feel him inside her thrusting, mating. . . .

"I think it's time for me to go." This had better be a great escape or Lord help her, she thought. She was ready to attack him on the spot.

She moved to get up, but Mike put his hand on her arm. "Sit down. I promised to be a gentleman, so you can be assured I won't throw you across the table and try to prove my theory, tempting as it may be. Besides, you haven't finished your tea and scones. You don't want to waste them, do you? Nothing you get in the States is quite like them."

She settled back in her chair warily, knowing he wouldn't allow her to leave. Besides, the man had come with her halfway across England. He wouldn't be deterred by a short walk back to the hotel to find her again. She took a bite of her scone and actually found herself savoring the crumbly muffin and sweet whipped cream.

He grinned at her. "Mom can't make them like that at home. Trust me."

That was what she was afraid of, she thought. She was beginning to trust him—even to like him. Somehow the big differences in their lives seemed of less importance at the moment. So did the idea of being a sabbatical fling. She caught hold of that crazy notion, not wanting it to wander farther into her heart.

"You look like a rabbit with a dog on its tail," he said. "Anything wrong?"

"That's a funny description and, no, nothing's wrong," she said, forcing herself to smile.

That he hit the mark so closely was disconcerting. The last thing she needed was for him to detect any sign of attraction on her part. She straightened her facial muscles into what she hoped was a neutral position and began to eat her scone again.

After the meal Leslie managed to stand up without him stopping her. Now she could escape. She opened her mouth to thank him, not that she knew what to thank him for—but it seemed appropriate.

"There's a little church across the bay in Saint Mawes," he said before she could speak. He stood and walked around the table to her. "Twelfth-century. Over five hundred years older than anything in the States. Think of all the history it's seen."

He made it sound so tempting, she thought, lured by the idea of seeing something so venerable. And clearly he knew what the sights were here in Cornwall. She hadn't even found her way to the basement of Pendennis Castle, for goodness' sake.

About twenty minutes later she found herself inside a tiny chapel, her footsteps ringing across the stone floor. A font carved completely from stone by Norman artisans sat under a high, narrow window, the sun streaming down upon it, bathing it in a beautiful yellow light.

Only Mike and she were inside. The only other person around had been a young man loitering at the bottom of the churchyard. He'd looked familiar, as if she'd seen him in other places, but she'd dismissed the notion. She was just a little paranoid and in truth nervous as a cat to be alone like this with Mike. Her brain was so scattered, she couldn't gather her common sense, and her body temperature was running between hot and hotter.

"The pews are more modern," Mike said into the hushed silence. "In medieval times people stood for the service, the nobles in the front, the common folk in the back. This area was first given to a Richard de Beaumont, to hold for William of Normandy, then it passed over in the sixteenth century to the Makefield family, who built the porch and hung the bell in the bellcote."

She whirled around. "How do you know all this?"

He held up a little pamphlet. "From this. The church puts it out. Most churches here do. You learn a lot about a country's past by reading one of these."

"Now I'm not so impressed."

"Hey, I found it and you didn't."

"You're wearing glasses and I'm not."

He made a show of adjusting them on his nose. "You just can't get over my brilliance in history."

"I thought you were a professor of literature."

He grinned. "I minored in English History. Love the stuff."

She grinned back. That blatant sexuality she'd experienced at the café seemed dampened here in the church, and she felt some of her equilibrium returning. Maybe she could cope with being alone in England—well, being without Gerry—and cope with Mike without feeling like some big predestiny was about to descend.

He continued. "I'm always intrigued by the notion of the people who stood in these churches, who they were and what their lives were like. I imagine them, try to conjure up their ghosts and see them here. It's easy to imagine you as one of them. I can see you in a veil and gown—"

"Now you're going to tell me I'd be a great nun."

He laughed. "You? Hardly. No, in the veil and gown of a noblewoman who knew her own mind and ruled with a gentle but iron hand. I doubt a lord would dominate a fingernail over you before you slammed him onto the right path."

"You make me sound like Attila the Hunness."

"Not even close." His voice dropped lower, and the way his eyelids shuttered half closed caught her attention. "He would go gladly because he'd be a fool not to. You're far wiser than he is, and he knows it. Besides, you're incredibly sexy when you're being logical."

The little church was suddenly an oven. And she thought she was safe from the physical attraction in here. Leslie fanned at her heating skin. "I think I'll go outside now."

She slipped out the door, grateful he wasn't between her and it. Lord knows what would have happened if he was. No one had ever called her sexy for being logical. In fact her ex had told her how predictable she always was.

Mike might have his good points, but, she told herself, sex wasn't everything. Not even great sex. It wasn't nearly enough for a relationship. And sex was all they would ever have together, because nothing else meshed between them.

She had to admit one thing, though. Despite all their differences, he was a fascinating man.

Showing off, that's what he was doing.

Mike admitted it cheerfully to himself as he and Leslie walked along the upper part of Falmouth Bay in a little quiet spot he'd found. He pointed out all the caves exposed by the low tide, which Cornish smugglers had used practically since the time the English Channel came into being. A pair of swans glided gracefully across the water, their cygnets trailing behind like a long kite's tail.

Leslie shaded her eyes with one hand and gazed out across the water, searching out the openings visible in the bay's low tide. She looked beautiful with the breeze playing through her dark hair, lifting and teasing the tresses framing her face. She didn't seem aware of the effect she had on men. Didn't she know? Hadn't anyone told her?

What a waste if they hadn't, Mike thought, but was delighted he'd be the first to open that door for her, for he intended to tell her often. Her defenses had been down that day, and it had been a pleasure to talk with her, to see her relaxing with him. If she still thought he was a masher, it certainly wasn't visible. In fact she seemed to enjoy his company.

He was definitely making progress.

He said, "Cornish smugglers have been glorified by fiction writers, mostly because of the French Revolution, when they ferried British spies and refugees across the channel. In reality they were brutal, especially in the eighteenth century, when they would kill the tax men who came to ferret them out or anyone who even looked to betray them. Knifings and hangings were a regular happening then. Like pirates, they weren't very glorious at all."

"You're bursting my bubble," she said, turning to him with a wry smile. "Who hasn't read Du Maurier's *Frenchman's Creek* or *Jamaica Inn*? Although *Jamaica Inn* did make the uncle, who was a smuggler, pretty nasty."

"They weren't nice guys by any means," Mike said. "But they were pretty ingenious in their methods."

"Oh!" She pointed to something out in the bay. "What's that?"

Mike peered at the water's surface, wondering what had attracted her attention. Then he saw the dark shape barely break the water. "A seal."

"Really? Do you know that in all the years I've gone down to the shore back home, I've never seen seals or dolphins or even a shark. Yet we're supposed to have them along the Jersey coast."

"Too many people and too much pollution. Mostly it's the pollution. Falmouth Bay is one of the three largest natural bays in the world, but it's cleaner than most."

"The things you know." She said it with a rueful tinge to her voice.

He had to laugh. "One of the occupational hazards of being in academia. We thirst for knowledge. I win Trivia games regularly."

"I did once against six people."

"Wow, I'm impressed."

She laughed. "Two of them were drunk, so I'm not sure it counts."

"A victory is a victory. So who is buried in Grant's Tomb?"

"Nobody."

"You pass." He grinned at her, liking the teasing that was growing between them. He wanted to reach out and touch her, draw her against his body, feel her breasts pressing into his chest. His chest, not his stomach. He wanted to see her lips swollen from their kisses. He wanted to strip away her clothes and caress her skin, find every spot that made her moan and writhe. He forced his hands to stay at his side. Progress came in baby steps, he reminded himself against the growing impatience. "What part of the shore did you go to?"

"Wildwood."

His grin broadened. "Me too. The place to be in my college days. See? It's fate for us to meet."

She really laughed this time. "Or sheer bad luck."

He didn't mind the words because the sunlight was bathing her in its richness, just as it had that old Norman font. If ever anything looked glorious, it was her happy and relaxed. Not able to resist, he stepped forward and kissed her.

Her mouth opened in surprise, and he couldn't help taking advantage of it. He plunged his tongue inside, tasting her honeyed sweetness.

At first she was reluctant to join in the kiss, but he coaxed her until she tightened her fingers in his shirt and touched her tongue to his. His blood slowed, pumping heavily, as his head spun from the headiness of the kiss. He drew her closer. Her breasts pressed into his chest, just perfect, just right, just as he'd known it would be. She moaned in the back of her throat, sending his senses into a silver-gray void of light and touch. The fantasy wasn't even close to reality.

He caressed her back, loving the feel of slender bones and feminine flesh. Her cotton sweater slid along her skin, tickling his palms and only adding to the overall kaleidoscope of sensations. Having her in his arms was like having a strawberry dipped in chocolate. Both were wonderful separate, but the combination was ambrosia. Leslie was ambrosia. Every bone in his body told him he hadn't been a fool to travel across the breadth of England for this.

He could have easily and happily kissed her forever, but a small voice inside him surfaced, reminding him of his gentlemanly pact with her. Reluctantly he eased his mouth from hers, but still held her close, even more reluctant to let her go completely.

" 'Nature is in earnest when she makes a woman,' " he said, quoting Wendell Holmes.

"What?" Leslie pulled herself out of his embrace.

"Nothing." He sighed. "I wasn't being a gentleman."

She looked away for a moment. "I didn't help matters."

He grinned. "Good, then we're even. Would you like to go up to Malpas for dinner? They have a good pub there. At least they did the last time I was here."

She shook her head. "I think I've had enough sightseeing for the day."

He thought he'd pushed his luck far enough for one day too.

They would just do Malpas tomorrow.

"Where is that damned key!"

Leslie kept one hand on her slipping bath towel and rifled through the outside pockets of Gerry's bag with the other. The key, which was supposed to be so conveniently stored, was nowhere to be had. All she'd come up with was an "Inspected by #23" scrap of paper. #23 probably had a better idea of where the key was than she did.

"Damn, damn, damn," she muttered under her breath as she went through the pockets one more futile time. She needed to dry her hair or else she'd look like Straw Woman, Queen of the Haystacks. It was bad enough there was no shower and she'd had to wash her hair while bending over the tub—an exercise designed to split stomach muscles from the rest of one's body—but no hair dryer! That was unthinkable. She'd been able to borrow one from housekeeping in the London hotel, but no such luck here.

That she didn't want to have a bad hair day in front of a certain male, she preferred not to think about too. Unfortunately she hated the thought of appearing in front of Mike looking like the Scarecrow from *The Wizard of Oz.* He confused her . . . and he made her feel special. Being pursued by a man was a novel sensation. She ought to be scared of him—there were crazy people out there—but she couldn't help feeling flattered by his attentions.

And his kisses . . .

She pushed the disturbing thoughts away. Very disturbing. But it was as if floodgates long shut were slowly opening. It was amazing what a man's declaration of attraction could do.

The phone rang. She snatched it up, hoping it wasn't the object of her latest thoughts, but Gerry, who would get an earful about the lost key. "Hello!"

No one answered.

Leslie frowned, automatically toning down her voice. "Hello? Hello?"

The line clicked off.

She pressed the receiver off-button to sever the line, then dialed O for the lobby. Mrs. Drago answered.

"My call was cut off," Leslie said. "Was that my friend Gerry? Did she say?"

"It was a he, dear, and, no, he didn't identify himself. He just asked for you."

"Oh. Could it have been Mr. Smith?"

"I can't put through room to room yet. And I don't believe he's gone out for the day. I'm sorry about your call."

"That's okay." Leslie smiled ruefully. "I was going to try to call back if you knew."

She hung up. Settling back on her haunches, unmindful of the water still dripping from her body, she stared at the closed bag, wondering if she'd have to take a knife to it to get it open. Then she realized the tiny lock was dangling only from the zipper. It wasn't slid through the other locking loop. The bag had been open the entire time.

This was another of Gerry's all-time dumb moves, she thought in disgust as she slid back the zipper. Granted, there was nothing of value in the bag, but Gerry must have completely flipped her common sense on this trip. How could she have left it unlocked like this?

Inside was the usual assortment of toothpaste, brush, deodorant, et cetera . . . but no portable hair dryer.

She cursed out loud, furious that Gerry had obviously forgotten to pack the hair dryer. So much for splitting up some of the essentials between them to save space and weight. "I never should have trusted her. On a lot of things!"

She wondered what a hair dryer cost in pounds and wondered just how useless an English one would be back in the States. The electrics were all different. And that was another thing, she thought. Gerry was supposed to have packed the travel adaptors too.

"Straw Woman, here I come," Leslie muttered, straightening and dumping the bag on the bed, half spilling out the meager contents. She went back in the bathroom to do what she could with her hair.

When she finally emerged, she was more irritated with her friend than ever. And even more so with herself. One of the things she admired most about Gerry was her joie de vivre. Gerry was not ruled by conventions and cautions. She gave to the world and took what it offered back in a cheerful manner.

She was paying now for Gerry's joie de vivre. She had no traveling companion and a string of bad hair days in front of her. She was unsensible enough to hate having bad hair days.

One of Gerry's "essentials" caught her eye, and she reached into the carry-on bag and pulled out a clear plastic bag that, oddly, had a book inside it. The book was pretty old and battered-looking, but not in too bad shape. Leslie tried to read the nearly indistinct gilt writing along the spine.

Pamela, or Virtue Rewarded.

Interesting title, she thought. It must be one of Gerry's old favorites. Gerry was always rereading books she enjoyed. This one sounded like a Regency romance.

She opened the bag along its resealing edge and took out the book, wrinkling her nose at the musty smell. She opened the cover carefully because of the book's poor condition. A faded memento was on the flyleaf:

To Abigail,
Wife and helpmeet forever after, on this our first day of marriage. My heart is with you always.
John

Who were Abigail and John? Leslie wondered. She'd never heard Gerry mention them. She guessed they were relatives, maybe an aunt and uncle who'd passed away and Gerry had gotten the book during the inevitable house clearing. It was nice that their love still lived, even if only in a book's flyleaf. Leslie turned the pages out of curiosity. The novel began with a letter from Pamela on her employment by a local lord. The pages felt as if they were crumbly, and she knew she ought to put the book back before it fell apart in her hands. But she found herself fascinated with the girl's first trials "below the stairs." Mike's words about Pendennis Castle came to mind, and she wondered if the girl had worried about keeping her footing on the narrow servant stairs. The language was archaic, but it flowed easily, drawing her into the story.

She couldn't help wondering what it would be like if she and Mike were playing virtuous maid and rakish lord. Those notions only created more notions, until she was envisioning the two of them on a bed together. Somehow Mike had turned into the virtuous one while she was ripping his clothes off his body.

No wonder Gerry reread the story, Leslie thought, finally putting the book aside. And she had better stop thinking about Mike and beds. This was becoming downright dangerous. Unfortunately she had a more pressing problem, and only one person could solve it for her.

Virtuous Mike.

She walked down the hallway, around the corner, and knocked on a door. Mike opened it, his eyebrows shooting up in surprise.

She grinned at him. "Where do I go to get a hair dryer?"

"I have one," he said.

She laughed. "I knew it. My hero."

FIVE

"What do you want a hair dryer for?" Mike asked, opening his door wider to admit Leslie. He pushed back his hair, still wet from his bath. "And why am I a hero for having one? Not that I'm complaining, just asking."

"Gerry was supposed to bring the hair dryer and she didn't."

"Oh."

After a moment's telling hesitation Leslie walked inside. Her top and jeans seemed to cling to her body, outlining her curves for his view. He reminded himself of his pledge to be a gentleman, although he decided chivalry stank. No wonder Twain had thought Walter Scott's work was for the birds. Unfortunately, take and the consequences be damned had its drawbacks too.

Leslie smoothed her hand over hair, bound in

a ponytail, drawing his attention to it. He frowned.

"What's wrong with your hair?"

She glanced away. "Gee, thanks. I'm doing the best I can."

"No, I mean it looks just fine the way it is."

"Really?"

He nodded. "I don't see that's it any—"

He paused, realizing that he was sailing into dangerous waters. If she thought her hair looked bad because she didn't have a hair dryer, then he'd better not say that it looked no different than usual to him.

". . . I don't see any *problem* borrowing my hair dryer," he finished, pleased with his cleverness.

"You're sure you don't mind?" she asked.

He shook his head. "I only use it when I'm in a rush, which is usually all the time. I tend to sleep in."

She glanced over at his bed, which dominated the small room. He imagined her in it . . . naked and inviting . . . her hair spilling across the pillow . . . the sheet barely covering her breasts. Would her nipples be pink or rosy in color? Or darker? He wanted to reach out and tug back the sheet, pulling it down her long, glorious length to reveal every inch of flesh to his gaze—

". . . so I think that'll be okay."

"Huh?" He stared at her, belatedly realizing she'd been talking to him about something mundane while he'd been fantasizing about her in his bed. He hadn't even gotten to the way her light scent would intoxicate him, or the way she would stretch against him, or the way she would . . .

He realized she was speaking again, and he still hadn't heard her words.

"What'll be okay?" he asked, trying to get himself under control. But his attention was taken with the way her collarbone curved gracefully along her shoulder. Delicate. Exquisite.

"My borrowing your hair dryer. Are you off in academia la-la land again?"

"Not even close." He grinned. "You never answered my other question, you know."

"What other question?"

"Why am I a hero?"

"Yes, I did. When I said Gerry was supposed to pack the hair dryer and didn't."

"But how does that make me a hero?"

"You have one to lend."

Sensible. It figured. He wondered what it was he was hoping to hear . . . that he had rescued her from some fate worse than death? Or that she couldn't live without his body? He liked that one. It was much, much better than heroic fame through hair-dryer possession.

She cleared her throat, clearly uncomfortable. "I think I'd better get going—"

He put himself between her and the door. "But you don't have the hair dryer yet."

"Oh."

He retrieved it from the bathroom, along with the adaptor for use in England. "You plug this into the wall, and this one into the one you plugged into the wall, and the dryer plug into the one you plugged into the one you plugged into the wall."

She smiled. "That sounds like your driving instructions."

"Just follow them and you won't melt out the dryer."

"Scary thought."

He handed over all the items in a heap, their fingers touching as they scrambled to make the transfer without dropping anything. Her skin was warm and smooth, like silk heated in the sun. He all but dropped the stuff he was holding in the overwhelming need to touch her more.

She managed to extricate her hands, the dryer, and its essentials before he could act on his impulse.

"I'll be careful," she promised, turning away from him.

"That's what I'm afraid of," he muttered.

She glanced over her shoulder. "What did you say?"

"Just commenting on the ironies of life."

He walked behind her to the door. With her hands full, it was up to him to open it. He put his hand on the knob, then turned to her.

"So what's on the agenda today? Would you like to see Land's End? We could drive up to

Tintagel, the ruins of the castle where King Arthur was supposed to have been born. *Last of the Romans, First of the Britons.* That was—"

"No." She shook her head. "I suppose I ought to explore around, but somehow . . ." She shrugged.

He looked her in the eye. "Gerry's not coming, Leslie, okay? She's in love, and in my experience people in love do crazy things, so you might as well enjoy your vacation."

"I intend to enjoy the rest of my vacation," she retorted, fire coming into her gaze. "And it has *not* been my experience that people do crazy things when they're in love."

"What planet are you living on? People travel cross-country for their lovers. They propose in front of millions of people at a ball game. They even marry while sky-diving. How can you say people in love aren't crazy? That sounds crazy to me."

"People marry the boy or girl next door, their high school sweetheart, their first love, the person whose lifestyle fits their own. Or they marry just because they have an urge to settle down, so they pick someone who also wants to settle down." She made a face. "That's hardly crazy behavior. In fact it's very sensible."

"Hells bells, woman," Mike exclaimed. "Don't you ever have a spontaneous moment in your life? Love is the greatest emotion we have. It's not something to be taken out and dusted off just because the next-door neighbor is the opposite sex and the right age. Carlyle says 'Love is ever the beginning of knowledge as fire is of light,' and Molière says 'Take love away from life and you take away its pleasures.' "

" 'What's Love Got To Do with It?' Tina Turner," she shot back.

"Everything," he replied, grabbing her by the arms and pulling her to him.

He kissed her.

Wildly and passionately he kissed her. Her mouth was rich and enticingly soft with promise. He could feel the hard edges of the plugs and dryer pressed between them, but he didn't mind. He ran his tongue along her lips, coaxing her more into the kiss. She resisted for an instant, then gave herself up to it completely, in the way he was coming to love. That total surrender was a seduction all its own, exploding all kinds of wants and needs inside him. What would the rest be like? He wanted more, always he wanted more. . . .

She pulled away, taking him by surprise. Panting, he stared at her, watching her draw in great gulps of air.

"This is sex," she said finally. "Physical attraction, that's all. And it's not enough."

"My God," he said. "Why are you so afraid?"

"I'm not afraid!"

He just stared at her again, letting the silence speak for itself.

"I'm not afraid."

He let out his breath in a frustrated sigh. "I'll pick you up in twenty minutes for Tintagel."

"I'm not—"

"You're going," he said, determined that she wouldn't hibernate any longer. "We'll talk about nice, light things only, but you're going." He opened the door. "Now, go finish getting ready."

She went out, glaring at him as she did.

He shut the door with a loud bang, wondering if she would actually be in her room when he got there.

She had better be.

She wasn't afraid.

Leslie forced herself to keep a careful eye on the narrow road through Bodmin Moor, ignoring the overly tall, very disturbing passenger next to her. She wasn't afraid, dammit.

That phrase had stayed with her all day long, though. It had made her actually wait for him to go on this trip, just to prove she wasn't. Then it had marred the magical ruins of Tintagel for her—even the harrowing walk up the hundred stairs to look down at the beautiful little cove that isolated the castle—because she couldn't get the damn thing out of her head!

Now she was driving back to the hotel, and it was still bugging her. She wasn't afraid. Was she?

Mike did make her feel nervous and off balance, she admitted. Sitting next to him like this was an exercise in restraint. *Her* restraint. All day, when she hadn't been focused on that damnable catchphrase, she'd found herself focusing on him. Admiring him. Feeling again the way his mouth had taken hers that morning. The gentleness and the demands of his kiss. She was always aware of his physical size, but also, even more, of his presence. She'd had a continual impulse to throw herself at him and make love. It had been all she could do to keep her hands off him. She felt like a boiler with the steam building up inside so tightly, she was about to blow.

"Interesting how Tintagel looks older than it is," Mike said, breaking the silence. "It was built in the twelfth century by an earl of Cornwall. King Arthur lived in the sixth. People believe there was another, older castle at the site—"

"I didn't read that in the pamphlet," she said, staring straight ahead.

"It wasn't in the pamphlet. I read it in a history of Cornwall years ago for a college course. Another myth busted. I hate when that happens."

"Me too."

Another thought about Tintagel occurred to her. She frowned, wondering if she should bring it up, then decided she should. At the very least it would keep her from fixating on his body. Those illicit thoughts were about to make her so crazy, she might pull over to the side of the road and pour herself all over him like molasses. How they'd manage in a car was the only thing holding her back. Control certainly wasn't.

She realized that her thoughts were right back where they'd been, and said forcefully to deter them, "Have you noticed anyone hanging around us?"

He frowned. "No. What do you mean?"

"Well, there was this guy I saw in Tintagel who I thought I saw when we were at that little church yesterday."

"We were alone in the church," he said. "Should I feel jealous that you've got your eye on some other guy?"

"No. I mean, that's not why I noticed him." She made a face, beginning to feel silly. "I just thought I saw a man today who looked like the same one I saw back in Falmouth."

"There are several facial types that you'll see reproduced over and over again here in England," he told her. "Any country, except probably ours because we're such a polyglot, have people who have the same physical traits. Hair color, eye color, tall and thin, short and plump. Whatever. You've probably seen several people with the same physical traits typical of Cornwall, and after your room being nearly broken into in London, you're probably overly wary."

"Paranoid, you mean." She couldn't help grinning. He had to be right because the other idea seemed so far-fetched. What did she have to offer a thief that would make him follow her all over England?

"I was trying to be nice," he said. "Stop being a 'fraidy cat. I'm here to protect you, aren't I?"

A little voice, that damnable, nagging little voice, came back just as it had all day, reminding her about what really scared her. It wasn't that this might only be a vacation fling for Mike. If her ex-husband, no prize in the excitement department himself, had thought she was too dull, then Mike, king of the impulsive, must think she was *extremely* dull. And if he didn't already, he soon would. How could he not?

And all his talk that morning about love . . .

A shiver went up her spine. Okay, so she was scared about more than Mike walking out on her because she was dull. But that didn't mean she had to be a slave to her fears. He'd asked her if she ever did anything spontaneously, spur-of-the-moment. She doubted it.

She spied a turnoff in the road up ahead. Bodmin Moor was pretty desolate—they had passed only a few cars on their way to Tintagel and none yet on the return trip—but the main road south ran straight through, if she remembered rightly. At least she didn't remember Mike making a turn through here on the way to Tintagel. The evening light had gone already, and she knew the sensible thing was to not be impulsive in strange surroundings.

But she had always done the sensible thing.

And it hadn't worked. Maybe it was time to try the impulsive. Just a little impulsive. She glanced over at Mike and knew she wasn't ready for the big time yet. One step past dull, though, maybe that she could handle.

The new road loomed up quickly.

She turned onto it, finding it to be a narrow dirt lane, just a track really. She slowed the car automatically to accommodate the sudden roughness of the roadbed.

"Wha . . . that's the wrong way!" Mike exclaimed, looking back behind him.

She shrugged as a surge of headiness pulsed through her veins. "So? We're here to see the sights, aren't we?"

"This is a moor! The only sights you'll see is more moor."

"Then we'll see more moor." She chuckled. "I thought you'd appreciate this. Or have you already seen Bodmin?"

"Well, no . . ." he began.

"Good. Then it'll be a treat to both of us."

"Not at night it won't."

"Aren't you the one who was advocating stopping to smell the roses?" she asked, becoming a little exasperated with his attitude.

"This isn't like you, Leslie. And that worries me."

"You don't know everything about me," she replied. "In fact you know very little."

"Okay. I'll shut up and enjoy the ride." He sat

back in the seat and folded his arms across his chest.

She supposed that was about as good as she'd get, but she still didn't understand what was bothering him. Lord knows, he would have made this turn in an instant.

The car plowed along slowly, the headlights illuminating only about twenty feet on either side. The grasses were wildly overgrown, with a sprinkle of color from the wildflowers interspersed in the green. She recognized heather and buttercups, but not much else in the dim light.

"This probably goes to a farmhouse," Mike said.

"Then we'll turn around when we get there." She glanced at him. "What's your hurry, anyway?"

"I . . ." He paused, then grinned. "I don't have one, do I? Lead on, Macduff."

"Shakespeare. I remember that from English class," she said, proud to have gotten at least one of his quotes. "Do you think I'll pass my English driving test if I make it through this road?"

"If you make it through this road and we don't wind up back in London, then you'll have passed your English *countryside* driving test," he replied, amusement in his voice. "The M roads are something else again."

"Jeez, you're tougher than my dad."

"That's not the relationship I had in mind, Leslie."

No kidding, she thought, and decided shutting up was the better part of valor. She didn't need to get her inner heat turned up right now. She had to get them through the moor . . . then she could cope with heat.

As they drove, the road seemed to spin out endlessly before them. Not a light was visible. In fact she could have been driving through pitch, it was so dark just beyond the car lights. Nothing crossed their path. Not a deer. Not a bird. Definitely not another car. Leslie's moment of spontaneity was beginning to give her a bad feeling.

"This must be some farm if the road to it is this long," Mike commented.

"We'll be fine," she said bravely. The one thing she wasn't at the moment was dull. She still kind of liked that. But they'd better come out somewhere soon.

Another turn loomed ahead.

What the hell, Leslie thought, and turned onto it.

This road was even more bumpy and overgrown.

"Ahh . . . hhh," Mike said warningly, sounding like he was thumping around inside a washing machine. "I think we're going north again."

"How can you tell?" Leslie asked, leaning over the steering wheel and trying to peer into the night sky. She couldn't see any stars, let alone one with directions on it.

"Watch, watch!" he said as they thudded into a pothole.

"Right." She returned her gaze to the track as she asked, "So how can you tell?"

"I have a good sense of direction. This feels north to me."

"But I turned right. We were going south, and I turned left. That was east. Then this road went to the right. That has to be south again. Right?"

"You're the driver." Out of the corner of her eye she saw him begin to pat his pockets, then stop. "I forgot," he said. "You don't like pipe smoke. The gods only know when I'll get a chance to smoke now."

She glanced over at him. "I never said I didn't like pipe smoke."

"Yes, you did. On the elevator that time."

"I remember that elevator ride very clearly . . ." Boy, did she ever. ". . . And I never said a word to you."

"But your face. The look on it . . ."

She chuckled. "It's illegal to smoke in an elevator. And the damn thing was so tiny. Can you blame me for being terrified?"

"No." He laughed. "And I was going to light up. I forget myself sometimes."

"No kidding, professor." She thought about all the reports about secondhand smoke, not to mention what it was doing to him, then decided to live dangerously. "You can smoke in the car. I don't mind, truly—as long as you open the window."

"Thanks. I have a feeling this is going to be a long trip." He got out his pipe paraphernalia, eventually getting a stream of smoke going to his satisfaction. He rolled down the window, but not before the smoky-sweet aroma of cherry tobacco filled the car. He added, "A real long trip."

She clenched her jaws, angry that he didn't appreciate what she was doing. The man was exasperating. She'd have thought he would have been impressed that she was following his advice for once. Instead he didn't like it that she was being impulsive. So much for changing one's stripes. Not when everyone else thought they were painted on with indelible ink.

Dammit, she thought, absently fighting the wheel as they bumped along. The night was beautiful, black and clear. She would enjoy this even if he didn't. And if he opened his mouth again, she'd shove that smoking pipe up his nose.

Leslie did enjoy the night . . . for about twenty more minutes.

A silvery haze in the distance caught her attention. As they drew closer to it, the haze seemed to take on a more solid shape.

Fog.

"From ghoulies, ghosties, and long-leggety beasties; And things that go bump in the night. Good Lord, deliver us!" Mike said.

"Who said that?" she asked.

"I don't know, but, boy, are they right!"

Leslie had her own moment of panic, then told herself to relax. All she had to do was stay on the track. As long as she did, it would eventually dump them out onto a tarmac roadway, and they'd be well on their way to Falmouth—and much farther south than Mike Smith had ever thought.

The fog met them a few seconds later, rolling over the car like a wispy white blanket. Occasional rents revealed the sky above. Leslie relaxed. This wasn't so bad.

But the farther they went, the only thing that changed was the fog. It got more dense, until it was like a thick curtain surrounding them. Leslie slowed the car to a crawl. No matter how much the vehicle parted through it, another curtain was waiting. Endlessly waiting.

Visibility closed in from twenty feet to five feet to no feet. Leslie could barely see the hood anymore. The illumination from the headlights, even the car's fog lights, was reflected right back, not penetrating at all. The only thing that did penetrate was the chill coming in Mike's open window. It seemed as if they were bumping along more than usual too.

"Am I on the road anymore?" she asked, trying to keep the desperation from her voice.

Mike opened the car door and looked down. "Barely. The verge is right here." He tapped his pipe against the bottom of the door edge, knocking the ash out. "I can't see anything else, but I think I can guide you this way."

"Make sure we stay on the track," she said. "Otherwise, to quote a wise man, Lord Peter Wimsey, 'Got lost in the fog and dropped in a bog.' "

"Wasn't that Sayers who wrote him?" Mike asked, surprising her that he even knew who Lord Peter Wimsey was. Clearly his question was rhetorical, because he went on. "She was a scholar really, doing a pretty decent translation of Dante's *Divine Comedy*. I believe she died before she could finish *Paradiso*, the final part of the trilogy—"

"Mike, just watch the damn road, or we really will drop in a bog!"

"We don't want to do that."

"No kidding."

As he went back to road watching, she shivered, half from the cold air and half from remembering the story in which Wimsey did drop in a bog and nearly got killed. She had a feeling no farmer would be around to drag her and Mike out.

Mike occasionally called out adjustments to her steering, interspersed with encouragement. They were going along nicely, until another worry came to Leslie's attention. She stopped the car and shut it off. It was as if the last light winked out on the world.

"What are you doing?" he asked. She sensed more than saw him straighten to look her way.

"We're down to a quarter tank of gas," she replied. "If we keep driving, we could run out of gas in the middle of nowhere, and we wouldn't be able to get out when the fog finally lifts. So I think we should stop and just wait it out."

"You're so logical," he said, slamming his door shut.

"Sure." She made a face. "That's why we're lost in the first place. I'm so damn logical."

"If it will make you feel better, I believe this is all a grand design on your part to get me alone and helpless and have your way with my body. The female version of running out of gas on a date."

She looked at him, terrified for an instant that that was what she really *had* done. Then she burst into laughter, positive that for all her wayward thoughts, she truly wouldn't have gone that far.

"Thanks a lot," he muttered. "My body's not that bad. Is it?"

She stopped laughing. His body was very good, but she wasn't about to tell him that. She didn't want to think about it, not with him so close, the two of them all alone . . .

"I'll never be impulsive again," she swore. "Look at where it got me."

"Alone on an English moor in the middle of the night with a man." He chuckled. "That's pretty good for a sensible girl like you. Hey, everyone ought to take an adventure from time to time. You just picked the wrong one."

"You can say that again."

"I would, but I don't believe in being redundant."

She shivered. "Is your window still open? I can't see that far. And if it is, would you shut it, now that you're not smoking? I'm a little cold."

"Sure." He rolled it up.

The fog somehow became even more impenetrable, something she would have thought impossible. But it lay on the windshield and side windows, as if the car were buried in a foot of snow. More eerily, the fog seemed to carry its own light, bathing them both in a weak glow.

"Does this fog seem normal to you?" she asked, sitting forward and peering at the white stuff.

"No. But English fog doesn't." He added, "It's amazing how fast this stuff comes on. Out of nowhere and so damned thick. This reminds me of Doyle's great story, *The Hound of the Baskervilles.* Remember when they were on the Gripen Moor, with everyone lost in a fog so dense, it was as if they were blind, and the hound of Hell was howling, hot on his prey, while Holmes and Watson searched frantically for the missing man before the murderer could get to him first. Great stuff Doyle wrote."

She shivered again, not at the cold this time. Trying to dispel the frightening images he'd just conjured, she began singing the Creedence Clearwater Revival song, "Bad Moon Rising."

Mike sang with her, his baritone blending nicely with her alto. Soon they were both fully into the song, the car bouncing in rhythm as they swayed back and forth in their seats. They were laughing when they were done.

"For our next selection," Leslie said, "we'll sing 'When the moon flies over Miami, I'll be a crescent for you.' "

"That can't be a real song!"

"Naah." She shook her head. "Just me being silly."

"I like it when you're silly."

"You do?" She shivered again, rubbing her arms and wishing she'd brought a sweater. England was much cooler in the summer than Pennsylvania's triple-H version: hot, hazy, and humid. At least she told herself this shiver had been from the cold again. It hadn't been anticipation.

"You need to warm up or you won't last the night," he said, glancing around the car. He was in shirtsleeves, too, so he had no jacket to offer her. He held out his arms. "Here."

She glanced over at him, raising her eyebrows. "Thank you, but no. I'll just stay here—"

"Afraid? Come on. I'll be a good boy. The console is between us, so I'll have to be a good boy." When she didn't move, he groaned. "Why do I look like a convicted serial rapist to you?"

She *was* cold, and she was being silly. But it

seemed just as foolish to take him up on his invitation, because she didn't trust herself. To reveal that, however, would tell a whole lot more about her emotions than she wanted him to know.

Very reluctantly she scooted over in the seat, leaning across the console to rest her upper body against his. She kept her arms wrapped around herself, creating an effective barrier to keep her breasts from touching his chest. But his arms came around her and drew her in tight to his frame. She could feel the heat emanating from him, warming her already—and warming her awareness too.

"See? This isn't so bad." He shook his head. "You could give lessons in puncturing the male ego."

"Somebody's got to do it."

The minutes passed endlessly, until time seemed to stand still. More than companionable heat began to seep into Leslie's senses. His chest was hard yet comforting as a pillow for her head. His arms held her loosely, yet the latent strength was waiting for a signal to come alive. His chin rested in her hair, as if it were the most natural place in the world. The scent of male and expensive cologne permeated deeply within her, imprinting themselves in some primitive way.

She realized how much she had suffered from touch deprivation over the last few years. As a female she needed to be held like this by a male, touched like this by a male. She needed the companionship that was being offered tonight. It answered some deep emptiness within her. So basic, the very fiber of her being cried out with satisfaction, saying, "At last." She hadn't felt its loss so keenly—until now.

She snuggled closer, liking what she was feeling. Being out alone on a moor in a terrible fog seemed less life-threatening now. It was just an inconvenience to wait out, that was all. That she was being dangerously impulsive by letting Mike hold her didn't matter against feeling another human being's concern for her, his caring. Gerry's premonition swirled around in her mind, which was growing ever more lazy with contentment. That premonition still seemed as silly as ever, but Mike holding her didn't. This was hardly impulsive. In fact it felt more and more like a sure thing.

As if by unspoken signal, he turned his head to look at her at the same time she turned to look at him.

Wanting more, needing more, she reached up and grasped his collar lapels, then pulled his mouth down to her's.

SIX

Mike's head reeled at the wildness of Leslie's kiss.

It wasn't what he'd expected. She was never what he expected, and that was part of why he stayed around. But her kissing him first . . . he was unprepared for that. This was the adventure for her that he had so wanted to see.

A vague caution surfaced in the back of his mind that he should stop this, but it paled against the feel of her, warm and inviting, in his arms. He wanted her to turn him into knots like this. He needed her to.

Her kiss became more demanding, her tongue thrusting to meet his, swirling together. The sensations pulled him into a fog deeper than the one just outside the car. They thrummed heavily along his veins, creating a tight ache that seduced him further. For that was what she was doin

Escape...

into Romance and embrace special savings.

Get 4 New Loveswept® Romances for just $1.99!

Plus FREE shipping and handling!

Get swept away by 4 New *Loveswept* Romances. Preview them risk-free—with no obligation and nothing to buy!

Keep them and Save $12.00! That's...

85% Off the cover price!

Get a FREE Gift!

To get your **FREE** personal lighted make-up case, peel off and affix this sticker inside!

Save 85% Off the Cover Price on 4 New *Loveswept®* Romances—

and Get a Free Gift just for Previewing them for 15 Days Risk-Free!

Imagine two lovers wrapped in each other's arms—a twilight of loneliness giving way to a sunlit union. Imagine a world of whispered kisses and windswept nights, where hearts beat as one until dawn. If romance beats in your heart and a yearning stirs in your soul, then seize this moment and embrace *Loveswept!*

Let us introduce you to 4 new, breathtaking romances—**yours to preview and to lose yourself in for 15 days Risk-Free**. If you decide you don't want them, simply return the shipment and owe nothing. **Keep your introductory shipment and pay our low introductory price of just $1.99! You'll save $12.00—a sweeping 85% off the cover price! Plus no shipping and handling charges!** Now that's an introduction to get passionate about!

Then, about once a month, you'll get 4 thrilling Loveswept romances hot off the presses—*before they're in the bookstores*—and, from time to time, special editions of select *Loveswept* Romances. Each shipment will be billed at our low regular price, currently only $2.50* per book—a **savings of 29% off** the current cover price of $3.50. You'll always have 15 days to decide whether to keep any shipment at our low regular price—but **you are never obligated to keep any shipment**. You may cancel at any time by writing "cancel" across our invoice and returning the shipment to us, at our expense. So you see there is **no risk** and **no obligation** to buy anything, *ever!*

Treat Yourself with an Elegant Lighted Make-up Case—Yours Absolutely Free!

You'll always be ready for your next romantic rendezvous with our elegant Lighted Make-up Case—a lovely piece including an assortment of brushes for eye shadow, blush, and lip color. And with the lighted make-up mirror *you* can make sure he'll always see the passion in your eyes!

Keep the Lighted Make-up Case—yours absolutely FREE, whether or not you decide to keep your introductory shipment! So, to get your FREE Gift and your 15-Day Risk-Free preview, just peel off the Free Gift sticker on the front panel, affix it to the Order Form, and mail it today!

*(Plus shipping and handling, and sales tax in New York, and GST in Canada. Prices slightly higher in Canada.)

Save 85% off the Cover Price on 4 *Loveswept* Romances with this Introductory Offer and Get a *Free Gift* too!

no risk • no obligation • nothing to buy!

Get 4 Loveswept Romances for the Introductory Low Price of just $1.99!

Plus no shipping and handling charges!

Please check:

❑ **YES!** Please send me my **introductory shipment of 4 Loveswept books,** and enter my subscription to Loveswept Romances. If I keep my introductory shipment I will pay **just $1.99—a savings of $12.00—that's 85% off the cover price, plus no shipping and handling charges!** Also, please send me my **Free Lighted Make-up Case** just for previewing my introductory shipment for 15 days risk-free. I understand I'll receive additional shipments of 4 new Loveswept books about once a month on a fully returnable 15-day risk-free examination basis for the low regular price, currently just $2.50 per book—**a savings of 29% off the current cover price** (plus shipping and handling, and sales tax in New York, and GST in Canada). There is no minimum number of shipments to buy, and I may cancel at any time. My **FREE Lighted Make-up Case** is mine to keep no matter what I decide.

PLEASE PRINT CLEARLY 20800 DA

NAME ____________________

ADDRESS ____________________

CITY ____________________ **APT.#** __________

STATE ____________________ **ZIP** __________

SEND NO MONEY!

Affix Your FREE GIFT Sticker

Prices subject to change. Orders subject to approval.
Prices slightly higher in Canada.

DETACH CAREFULLY AND MAIL TODAY!

Get 4 Loveswept books for the Introductory Low Price of just $1.99! And no shipping and handling charges!

Plus get a FREE Lighted Make-up Case!

You risk nothing—so act now!

INTRODUCTORY OFFER!
SAVE 85%
OFF THE COVER PRICE!

NO POSTAGE
NECESSARY
IF MAILED
IN THE
UNITED STATES

BUSINESS REPLY MAIL
FIRST CLASS MAIL PERMIT NO 2456 HICKSVILLE, NY

POSTAGE WILL BE PAID BY ADDRESSEE

Loveswept®

Bantam Doubleday Dell Direct, Inc.
PO Box 985
Hicksville NY 11802-9827

DETACH CAREFULLY AND MAIL TODAY!

seducing him in her innocence and in her honesty.

He thrust his fingers into her hair, the silken strands sliding along his palms. He tilted her head up, taking her mouth harder, trying to tell her with his kiss all that he was feeling inside.

She moaned in the back of her throat, her arms wrapping around his shoulders, holding him tightly, as if she would drown if she did not. Her nails dug into his skin through the thin shirt, inflaming him all the more.

He pulled his mouth away to spread kisses on her jaw, her neck, her cheeks, her eyes, her forehead . . . everywhere he could kiss. He buried his lips in the hollow of her throat, feeling her pulse beating frantically. He created that excitement in her, he thought, touching the spot with his tongue.

She moaned again, her arms tightening. Mike succumbed to the response, pushing away her blouse, the buttons popping open, so that he could rain kisses on her soft, satin flesh. He traced the tops of her breasts, just the edge of the roundness above her bra. The lacy material was a wisp that scratched slightly along his chin.

Already he was frantic for her and he didn't know how he would exert any control over himself. Especially when her hands squeezed between them, fumbling with his shirtfront. The cool air hit his exposed skin as she got it open to his waist, but her palms were warm as they pressed against his chest, burning away the chill. They skimmed along his torso with the touch of a butterfly's wing. So light yet so intoxicating.

"God, don't stop," he murmured. His own fingers felt like they were filled with lead as he tried to unhook her bra. Finally he stripped it from her, taking her blouse with it. Her breasts were cool as he kissed first one, then the other, but her nipples were hard and hot on his tongue. She arched herself against his mouth, her fingers threaded through his hair and pulling him impossibly closer. He kissed and swirled and nibbled with lips and tongue and teeth until she was moaning and writhing in his arms, her hands digging and clinging and touching, demanding him to take the torment further. He was happy to oblige until he thought he would burst.

He raised his head finally, drawing air into his starved lungs. He kissed her with such passion that he realized he was being rough and tried to temper it. But she was almost biting at his lips, her arms so tight around his neck that what little air he had taken in had small chance of coming out again.

He didn't care. She was matching him want for want, need for need. That was all that mattered. He pressed her breasts into his chest, not worrying if she would break in his embrace. She wouldn't. He would break in hers first. The feel of flesh to flesh was unbearable, and he wanted more.

"The console," she gasped.

"I know." He swallowed, managing a moment of rational thought. "Maybe we should stop now—"

"No!" Leslie clung to him harder. "No."

"Thank God." Never had he been so grateful as in that moment. He hadn't known how the hell he would stop this; it was like a tidal wave of emotions and sensations, tossing him in its wake. He pulled her across the console, trying to help her get her long, long legs across the hump. They wound up in a tangle of arms and legs and laughter.

"I'd say something about a bed being more sensible," he said, "but that's your job."

"That's no fun," she poo-pooed, her breasts jiggling delightfully as she tried to settle her legs on either side of him. He captured one in his mouth, while running his hands up her thighs, those gorgeous sleek thighs, raising her skirt nearly to her waist. The thin material hiding the most intimate part of her from him was silk, beautiful, touchable silk. He stroked her softly, gently, incredibly gratified at the shudder that went through her.

"Oh, Mike, oh, Mike," she chanted. "We need more room."

She leaned forward, one hand reaching past him to between the seat and the door.

"Wha—" he began.

His seat back suddenly flew backward, taking

him and her with it until it was stopped by the rear seat. Mike found himself lying flat with Leslie on top of him, the wind knocked from his lungs. She pulled herself up, dragging her breasts across his chest. Mike decided he was about to die a happy man as she settled the length of herself, breast to chest and hips to hips, with him.

"That's better," she murmured, kissing his jaw.

"I'll say." He trailed his palms up the back of her thighs and around her derriere, slipping his fingers under the silk panties to knead the soft flesh.

She moved against him in response. She was incredible, just incredible. But he'd known that. The first time he'd felt her body against his, in that elevator, he'd known it would be like this. All flame and need between them. He stroked her until she was a wild thing, biting and clawing, driving him nearly insane.

"Mike, please," she moaned, kissing him frantically. "Do you have . . ."

He knew instantly what she meant. "My wallet."

He lifted his hips, pressing himself into the intimate cradle she created and nearly losing himself in the process. By some miracle he got his wallet out and found the small package, credit cards flying around the car's interior. Leslie already had his clothes half off, and she took over the task of protection. Sweat beaded his forehead at her touch. He couldn't stand it, he thought, realizing he hadn't even begun to imagine what she could do to him.

Somehow he got that wisp of silk off her body. She sank down on top of him, sheathing him slowly and completely. He gasped out her name, closing his eyes and forcing himself to restraint against exploding from the pleasure. She moved against him, rising above him with each stroke. He met her and matched her, thrusting himself faster and faster into the warm, moist velvet that clasped him so perfectly. He was vaguely aware of the roughness of the seat fabric against his back and the car wall along his side. The annoyances faded against the almost painful rushing sensations that shot through him as Leslie arched against him, moaning in satisfaction. In that instant, emotions buried themselves deeply within him, yet spun out to twine themselves with hers, binding him to her in a way that was unbreakable.

Quickly, all too quickly, everything faded into a warm blackness that harbored only her and him against the fog. Against the night. Against everything.

Together.

Light penetrated Leslie's dozing. She became aware of the painful numbness in her legs. Her arms were cramped against her sides, and her face was smashed against something warm and hard.

Her back was freezing. She realized it was daylight, she was lying on top of Mike, and she was wearing only a cotton skirt—around her waist.

The night came back in a rush.

She groaned in horror, trying to rise up and cover herself at the same time. What had she done in her zeal to prove herself impulsive? She knew. She knew all too well. Her lips felt puffy and bruised, and she was sore in the most intimate of places.

Mike grunted and shifted in his sleep, nearly waking up. Wanting to get out of this position before he did wake, she stilled for a moment, waiting for him to return to a deeper sleep. She couldn't help wondering how a man his size had slept at all in the cramped car, let alone with her on top of him. The thought brought back memories, sharp and vivid, of the night before. Of them making love more than once. She had never been a one-night stand before. She had never opened her emotions so much before. She let out a little cry of despair, knowing she'd become exactly what she didn't want. A sabbatical fling, a woman who had been desperate to prove she wasn't dull and that she was destined to be with him. Only there was more to it than that—for her.

His breathing deepened again, drawing her attention. Grateful to set her emotions aside, she carefully rose up while reaching around to try to find her blouse. A movement outside caught her eye, and she stared open-mouthed through the driver's-side window at the road about a hundred yards away. Cars and trucks whizzed along it with the morning traffic. She had been so close to salvation. So close.

She glanced away only to find a face pressed close to the passenger window. She screamed, crossing her arms over her bared breasts and scrambling back into the driver's seat, hitting the horn with her hip. The curious cow mooed in distress, backing away and bumping the car in the process. Mike shot upright.

"What? What?" he demanded, glancing around in confusion.

"It's morning," Leslie muttered, her face heating as she caught an intimate glimpse of his body. She realized she was sitting on her blouse, so she grabbed it up, thrusting her arms into it and buttoning it with as little exposure as possible.

"Morning?" Mike peered outside the car. "By damn, it is. Hey! There's the road. And it isn't the road on the northern edge of the moor. That was a two-lane road. This must be the A-Thirty-eight. How about that, Leslie, you were almost to the other side."

She groaned again. "Yes, I noticed."

"Good job." He leaned over and kissed her cheek before she could twist away. "Next time I'll be more confident. Oh, Lord, am I stiff—"

She gasped, then realized he was talking about the condition of his entire body. Her face flamed again with embarrassment, her cheeks so hot, she felt she'd burn her fingers if she touched them. He stretched immodestly, casually pulling up his pants. He started to chuckle.

"You amaze me, woman," he said. "A cow field for a romantic interlude. Good thing they weren't around last night—"

"Can we go now?" she asked in desperation, wanting only to find her bed, pull the covers over her head, and forget what had just happened.

He stopped laughing. "Are you all right?"

"Yes, I'm all right. Can we go now?"

"You're not all right."

"*I'm all right,*" she repeated sternly, while trying to slip her feet into her dockers.

"Oh. I've forgotten." He leaned over the console and tried to put his arms around her.

She shied away. "What do you think you're doing?"

"I thought I was going to kiss you good morning."

"You did that already."

He snorted. "What the hell is wrong with you, Leslie?"

"This was a mistake, okay?" she snapped, turning on the car. The motor roared to life. She jammed it into gear with a jerk, and the car began to pick its bumpy way among the cows milling on the dirt road.

"This was no mistake," he said. "You wanted

it as much as I did. Maybe it wasn't in a proper bed, but—"

"Mike, dammit! It was . . . too impulsive."

"It wasn't impulsive. It was necessary."

"Necessary?" she scoffed, finally finding the turnoff for the main road. "What happened between us was hardly necessary. I'm not interested in having a vacation fling . . . or being your sabbatical one."

"Lady, you really do amaze me. You're running again. How the hell you can turn it on like you did last night and then turn it off so completely this morning . . ." He ran his fingers through his hair. "Forget it. Just forget it."

"That's my point," she replied, while wondering what her own hair looked like. Probably like she'd been making love all night. How could she have been so lacking in common sense last night? She had given herself so intimately to him, not even thinking about how easy it would be for him to walk away. Trust came over time with a man, and so should making love. Worse, she'd practically thrown herself at him after that first kiss. This was her fault, her lapse of integrity.

"I suppose you want to forget this too," Mike said, holding up her panties, just as she reached the turn onto the main highway. Mortified, she snatched them out of his hand and managed to get them on without showing more than thigh. She hoped.

He made a choking noise. She ignored it.

The car ride to the hotel was made in awkward silence. Further embarrassment awaited them on their arrival, when Mrs. Drago accosted them as they came through the front doors.

"Oh, my dears, I thought you'd had a crash when you didn't come in last night!" she exclaimed loudly, over the breakfast-service clatter.

"We just got caught in the fog," Mike said smoothly.

"Yes, it was nasty last night. That's why I worried, you being American and not used to driving in it."

"We're fine," Leslie managed to mutter before practically scurrying away, positive every single person there knew that she and Mike had made love.

When she reached her room, she shut the door behind her and leaned against it. The world was shut out finally.

Leslie sighed. What a night. She had been taken to the heights of ecstasy and plunged into the depths of despair. Mike had accused her of running again. He was right. She was running, from him. What she felt for him had come on too fast, was too deep, and if she continued, she'd be in too far to avoid the inevitable pain. And it was inevitable. He was a man, and men left her. She wasn't ready to expose herself to that again.

Maybe he would go now, she thought, since he'd gotten what he'd wanted from her. Pain squeezed at her heart. She forced the sensation away, knowing the longer this went on, the more she would hurt later. Better he left now.

Mentally stiffening her spine, she straightened from the door and walked over to the mirror to assess the damage. She moaned in despair at the give-away tangle of her hair. Her breasts were clearly unbound under her blouse. Her bra must still be in the car. But it was the mascara flakes under her eyes and the hooded look to her lids that spoke volumes about the night before. Her face heated all over again. So unsensible. So *incredibly* unsensible.

She got herself into the bath as fast as she could, allowing herself to luxuriate in the soothing warm water. But it didn't last long as images, touches, tastes, and smells of her and Mike together invaded her mind over and over again.

She got out of the bath, giving up on it as a relaxer, and after drying off, tried the bed instead. After all, she was behind on sleep.

She opened *Pamela*, hoping a little reading would settle her mind. It usually worked when she was overly tired. Her stomach felt empty, too, but not enough for her to leave the room. Nope, nope. She was staying in here until she got all these confusing, disturbing emotions under control. A little sleep would bring her worlds closer to that goal.

Pamela, it turned out, was having her first encounter with her dissolute lordship. The young maid fended him off finally, keeping her virtue intact for the time being.

Leslie slammed the book closed. "Pamela—one. Leslie—nothing."

She rolled over and tried to sleep.

It was impossible.

Leslie had come to her senses far too soon.

Mike cursed under his breath as he tried to decide whether he'd given her enough time to calm down.

He still couldn't understand why what they had done was so upsetting to her. Even she didn't deny how wonderful their lovemaking had been. So why the hell was he in the bar and she in her room? Because he was leaving her alone for the moment so that she could cope. And he was leaving her alone because he was angry with her too.

"The bar's not open yet, sir, but I'll be happy to get you something."

Mike smiled at Mr. Drago, who stood in the bar's doorway. In the few days they'd been here, it was obvious that sweet, fussy Mrs. Drago ran everything else, while the bar was the mister's domain. It was the only place Mike had ever seen him. "Just a mineral water. Mostly I came in because the door was open and the place was deserted."

"Righto." Anyone else would probably ask out of curiosity what the problem was, but Mr.

Drago had his own ideas on how barmen should be. He went behind the bar and got Mike his drink, then left, all without a word.

Mike eyed the fizzing clear liquid in his glass . . . the fizzing, clear, *warm* liquid. Although more and more English places were providing ice in the American way of serving drinks, it still wasn't universal.

Mike picked up the glass and took a healthy swallow. Yep, he thought. It tasted just like Alka-Seltzer.

He just sat for a while, wondering if he should pack up and head out for Cambridge. But he couldn't help feeling that the aftermath was his fault. In a car, in a cow pasture, within view of a major roadway. Hell, no wonder she was embarrassed and upset. And she hadn't been ready to make love, not really. He knew that. He'd always meant to do a little old-fashioned wooing before ending up in a very comfortable, very private bedroom. Of course they could find that bedroom at a later time. And time would take care of her emotional readiness.

The real problem was this whole notion of her being a sabbatical fling. How could he prove she wasn't if he left for Cambridge now? And even if he didn't, *she* would be going back home shortly herself. He would have to stay on then, to do his work. How to convince her he'd be coming back to her? Faith and trust just didn't have an opportunity to develop in the short time they'd be together.

An hour later he was still nursing his bromide disguised as a fashionable drink and still wondering how something so beautiful had turned so disastrous. The only way to fix it—confronting her—also seemed to be the best way to have his ego tromped and stomped. But as Terence said, "Fortune favors the brave." He also reminded himself of one of the tenets of Tang Soo Do karate: No retreat in battle.

Finally feeling buoyed to face her, he headed out to the lobby, waving at Mrs. Drago, who was registering a new guest, a youngish man who looked somehow familiar. Mike shook the notion off, took two steps toward the stairs, then turned and went out the front doors instead.

"No sense going without ammunition," he muttered, glancing over his shoulder as he headed toward the flower garden. No one was around. With his penknife and a twinge of guilt as accomplices, he divested Mrs. Drago's garden of a small bouquet of carnations, roses, daisies, and lavender. Not wanting to be caught flower-handed, he took the outside stairs to the second floor. Once inside the hotel again, he went straight to Leslie's door. He gazed at the blue-painted wood, then took a deep breath and knocked.

"Who is it?"

Mike figured she probably already had a good

idea of who it was, so he said, "I just want to talk with you."

"I don't think that would be a good idea."

Mike decided social embarrassment had its place in the world. "Leslie, if you don't let me in, I'll stand out here and pound on this door until you do."

He was about to repeat his threat when the door finally opened. Leslie peeked out. He thrust the flowers at her. "These are for you."

She made a face, but took the flowers. "Where did you get them?"

"Don't ask."

"See? That's the whole problem. If I were to pick 'don't ask' flowers for you, you'd probably have an allergy to them."

He frowned. "But I'm not allergic to flowers."

"No, of course you're not. That's why I didn't pick them."

He felt he was being sidetracked from their problems. "Can we talk?"

"I see we're quoting Joan Rivers now." She sighed. "Really, Mike, it won't do any good."

"I think it will. I know everything was wrong last night about our making love and this morning—"

"Mike!" She practically snapped his name at him, glancing to her right. "There are people."

He looked over at the family of four making their way down the hall. He turned back and smiled. "This is why you should let me in, so that we can have a conversation without being overheard."

"Can't you just go away?"

"No."

She set her jaw so visibly, he thought she wouldn't let him in. But then she opened the door wider. He stepped inside, trying not to grin at his success.

Her bed was mussed, as if she'd tried to get some sleep.

"I was just dressing for dinner," she said, pushing the door against the edge of the sill but not clicking it shut. She was wearing a skirt and top, with her hair pulled back. His hands itched to touch her again, to feel her in his arms, writhing against him in need. He suppressed the urges as she added, "I've got your hair dryer for you—"

"Keep it."

"No, really."

"Keep it. You need it."

"Gee, thanks."

"I didn't mean it like that," he said. "It's just that you don't have yours, so go ahead and use mine. I don't need it. Anyway I'm not here for the damn dryer. Leslie, last night wasn't what I wanted it to be . . . I mean, it wasn't where and how we should have been making love."

"It wasn't making love, Mike. It was sex. Purely physical."

"It was a helluva lot more than that!" he said hotly. "It—"

"I'd better find a glass to put these in," she interrupted, sweeping into her bathroom.

He was losing the battle fast here.

No retreat, he thought, forcing himself to gather his thoughts. Her reading book on the nightstand caught his eye. Curiosity won out temporarily over retreat, and he picked up the book, its page marker a hotel brochure. He realized instantly that it wasn't a beat-up book but a truly old book. It had slightly smaller dimensions than was now fashionable in hardbacks; vellum was used on the outside cover; the slight brittleness was a signal of rag-mixed paper. This was a very old book in fairly good condition actually. He looked at the spine to find that it was Richardson's *Pamela*. That Leslie was reading the book itself surprised him. Usually people didn't read old, old books, because of the great potential for damage. Curious.

Like any book lover, he caressed the worn backing, then opened the flyleaf. His hands shook when he read the inscription. He knew this book and it was no ordinary book. It was the Adams. Leslie was the owner of the Adams? An odd thought nudged at him that this wasn't right. But he had the proof in his hands. Was she crazy carting the thing all over England like this? And reading it! Didn't she know what body oils could do to the pages?

"Leslie, my God, woman!" he exclaimed as she emerged from the bathroom. "Have you lost your mind? This is history! History! You don't treat it like this!"

"Treat what like this? What are you talking about?" She was staring stupidly at him.

"The Adams!" he said. "You have the Adams!"

SEVEN

"What Addams? Why are you frothing at the mouth?" Leslie asked, bewildered by Mike's frantic gestures. One minute he was trying to talk about a futile cause, namely their nonrelationship, and now he was ranting about an Addams. What did Gomez and Morticia have to do with anything?

"What Adams! What Adams! Leslie, come on!" He put the book on her bed and gently wiped the cover with a corner of her bedsheet. "You know exactly what I'm talking about. This is Richardson's *Pamela*—"

"Yes, I know. I've been reading it."

"Yes, and I can't believe it! Do you know what you can do reading this?"

She walked over to him. "Become a maid in a manor house?"

He frowned at her. "You really don't know what I'm talking about, do you?"

"Half the time I don't. Which is half the problem."

"Your fingers and hands have dirt and body oils that can destroy the vellum and paper. Not to mention just leaving it out for anything to spill on it! This should be under glass somewhere. It's over two hundred years old."

"Two hundred!" She stared at him in amazement. "How the heck can you know that?"

"Because it's the Adams!" His exasperation came across the room at her like a tidal wave. "You must have paid a fortune for this—"

"I didn't pay anything," she said. "It's Gerry's. And what is this Addams business?"

"Gerry's!" He sat down on the bed. "Then she's got a collector's book of rare proportions."

Leslie frowned. "That doesn't sound like Gerry."

"I don't understand. This is an original edition of Richardson's *Pamela*. It's considered the first modern romance novel. That's one thing. But this particular book was a wedding gift from John Adams to his wife, Abigail—"

"John Adams!" she exclaimed, a tremor of panic shooting through her. "As in the second U.S. president, John Adams? And Abigail, the First Lady?"

"I'm not talking Bill and Hillary here. Yes, that John and Abigail Adams." Using a corner of the sheet, he opened the book to the flyleaf and pointed at the inscription. "See?"

"But I thought they were relatives of Gerry's," she whispered, sinking down onto the mattress as her legs turned to rubber. "And I thought you were talking about Gomez and Morticia Addams, with two *d*'s."

"Not hardly. This book isn't a household fact, like Jefferson signing the Declaration, but it's known in collector circles. There's a colleague of mine at Temple who would kill for this. That's how I heard about it."

"But what the heck is Gerry doing with it?"

"Is she a collector?"

Leslie shook her head, still feeling unnerved. "Only of Annalee dolls. She reads all the time, though. But I'd know if she were collecting something like this. Even if she were collecting books, she couldn't afford to collect rare and valuable ones like this. I mean, it's got to be worth a fortune!"

"It's a piece of history, Leslie," Mike said, reverently closing the book cover. "It's a wonderful, beautiful piece of history about the lifelong love and devotion of two people for each other."

"So how did Gerry get it?"

"Can you call her to find out?"

Leslie gritted her teeth, jumping to her feet. "I don't have a phone number where she is! She was in a hurry when she called here, and I was so damn mad, I never even asked." She pushed her anger away and thought for a moment. "I can't even remember the guy's name. Toomey . . . Terry . . . I don't know! She probably inherited this Adams book and didn't pay any attention to what she had. The first part I can't even imagine. I don't know of any relatives of hers who are relations of the Adamses. I don't even think she has any in Massachusetts. But not treating a rare book properly . . . that would be just like Gerry." She frowned. "Although it was in a sealed plastic bag in her suitcase."

"Get it and we'll put it back in."

She got the bag from the carryall. Mike took it from her and carefully slipped the book inside, sealing and resealing the opening until he was satisfied that the bag was truly safe against all elements and mishaps.

"There," he said, then sighed. "The Adams. I can't believe I'm holding it."

Somehow it was annoying to see him fawning all over a book, herself forgotten. Leslie decided she was being foolish. This should be what she wanted. Yet it hurt that he could turn himself on and off like this.

"I'll see if the hotel has a safe for its guests," she said, feeling she was back to being sensible.

"I doubt it does."

A call to the lobby confirmed he was right. Leslie hung up the receiver to find Mike caressing the plastic-bagged volume exactly the same way he had caressed her.

Gently . . . sensually . . . lovingly.

Anger, sudden and intense, boiled up inside her at having been so quickly dismissed by him. And for a book. A damn book.

"Keep it!" she snapped.

"What?" He looked up at her, bewildered.

She realized how much of her own emotional state she'd just revealed to him. And to herself.

"I said for you to keep it in your room for now," she muttered, knowing the book was better off with him anyway. He understood its worth far better than she. "I'll just be tempted to finish reading it if it's in mine."

"You certainly don't want to do that," he said, then grinned. "I'll go put it safely in my room until we leave."

"Until *you* leave," she said even lower under her breath. But he was already out her door. Racing down the hall, no doubt, to drool over the Adams. A *Playboy* centerfold probably wouldn't turn him on as much.

Leslie drew in a deep breath and shook herself. What did she want? What did she expect? This only confirmed that his interest in her was fleeting.

"Speaking of fleeting," she muttered, deciding not to be there when, or if, he came back.

She picked up her purse and headed downstairs, forgoing dinner in the dining room, where Mike was bound to show up, for the nicest pub she could find within walking distance.

Leslie wasn't at dinner.

Mike frowned as he left the dining room, absently waving his thanks to Mrs. Drago. He'd gone back to her room only to find she'd already left. He'd expected her to be down here. One of the other guests assigned to their table mentioned she'd seen Leslie leave the hotel earlier. He'd immediately gotten up and checked on the car. It was still parked where they'd left it. He considered trying to track her down wherever she was in town, but realized it for the futile gesture it would be. Her luggage was here, her car was here, The Adams was here. She'd be back.

Why had she left, though? He hoped it was only because Mrs. Drago was serving three-day-old gâteau drenched in cream and Leslie preferred her cake fresh.

After dinner he stepped outside to smoke and to wait for her. He puffed on his pipe, getting the tobacco glowing with ease and savoring the taste of smoky cherrywood swirling around his mouth. The sun was just about below the horizon, its red-gold glow turning a gentle gray-blue in those few moments between sunset and nightfall. Several stars were already visible in the sky. The air was quiet. No breeze stirred the leaves. Mike sighed at the beauty of it all. And more.

The Adams.

It was beautiful, he thought, still not believing

he'd touched such personal antiquity. Like Jonson's notes to Shakespeare, that inscription was the joy of the whole thing. He wondered how many times Abigail Adams had read it during the course of her marriage. It must have been a keepsake. Had it helped sustain her when she was separated from her husband? Had Adams been telling them both something with that book, that their virtues of love, conscience, and integrity would have their own reward? Had it sustained the husband on lonely nights to know his wife had the book, a reminder of his love and faithfulness?

Fascinating, Mike thought, smiling happily. Then he frowned. Why wasn't Leslie back yet?

Falmouth was pretty safe, but he still didn't like the thought of her wandering around alone after dark. And they had things to settle between them. The discovery of the Adams had sidetracked him. He wondered if all these obstacles were a curse put on him by Cupid. Time was short, and he was always dropping one step back for every two steps forward with her. However, she'd entrusted him with the Adams. That was a good sign.

The object of his thoughts came into view, trudging up the drive. Mike smiled and walked down to meet her.

"You didn't tell me you were going out for dinner," he said. He was careful not to touch her, realizing he'd have to go slowly with her.

"I didn't know I had to," she replied, not looking at him.

Her tone wasn't frosty, but he felt a bite all the same.

"You didn't," he agreed. "I didn't mean to rush you into anything last night, Leslie—"

"You didn't." She glanced at him, then away. "I take responsibility for my actions. I realize I could have said no, and if I had, you would have . . . well, you wouldn't have . . . nothing would have happened."

"That's right," he began eagerly, glad she was seeing how he felt about her.

"You don't have to rub it in."

He frowned. "Rub what in?"

"That it was all my fault. That I was the local trollop—"

"Leslie! How can you say that about yourself?" he demanded, appalled that she would even think such a thing. "And what the hell does that make me? The local trolloper? Don't turn what we had into something tawdry."

"In the car in a cow pasture?" She snorted. "Mike, I think we just wrote the book on tawdry."

"It was only spontaneous and wonderful, dammit."

"You don't sound like it was."

"Not with you trying to make it into *Taxi Driver*. I'm going to have to do something about your prudish attitude."

She halted at the bottom of the hotel steps, holding up her hand. "Please, Mike. Let's not argue about this. It was a mistake, that's all. Just two ships passing in the night who heard the same foghorn."

"Sex is not some damn foghorn," he snapped.

"And it's not making love either."

She walked up the steps and inside the building. He followed her. Even in his anger he couldn't help admiring her slim, straight back and curving derriere.

"What are you doing?" she asked, turning around when they were halfway up the inner stairwell.

"What are *you* doing?" he asked, instead of replying.

"Going to my room."

"And I'm going to mine. Which is right down the hall from yours, remember?"

"I hate it when you win an argument."

Mike smiled as they continued the journey in silence. He wished he knew how to convince her that he really did care. But how could he say it better than he already had? Time was against him unfortunately, and that was what was really needed here. Just plain old time to get to know each other better.

As they reached her room, he had a strong urge to try to persuade her again that her way of thinking was all wrong. He decided not to, however. He'd probably pressed enough as it was.

Maybe a good night's sleep was all she needed to regain her perspective. This wasn't a retreat from battle, just a regrouping. His only worry now was whether she'd take off during the night. He decided to put in a word with the Dragos to let him know immediately if Leslie checked out.

"Good night," she said as she opened her door.

"Good night," he said, passing by her.

He got two steps beyond when he heard her gasp, "Oh, no!"

He turned around and came back, a knot twisting in his stomach. He glanced into her room . . . and his jaw dropped in astonishment. It looked as if the room had been turned upside down. Her drawers were opened, clothes hanging out. Her luggage was in a jumble. Chairs were turned over. The sheets had been yanked off the bed, and the mattress itself was askew.

"Did you have a fight with your room while I was gone?" he asked.

She gave him a look that would freeze hell. Mike decided further humor wouldn't help the situation. She turned back to the mess. "I don't believe this! Twice in one trip!"

"This time they got in," he commented. "England isn't known for a high tourist crime rate, but their unemployment is up. Not having a job turns people desperate. Better check to see what's missing, such as your money or passport or jewelry."

"I have my money and passport with me, but no good jewelry to speak of. I left most of it at home and brought decent costume stuff. Except for my diamond studs." She shivered in reaction. "I feel violated."

He took off his jacket and put it around her, squeezing her shoulders in the process. He hated to see her so vulnerable and hated whoever had put her in this state. Much as he wanted to punch something, he said soothingly, "I know. You've had some bad luck here."

"I'll never leave home with or without my American Express card again," she said. "Because I'll never leave home again!"

"I'll bring the world to you," he said, glad that she was making a joke. "You need to look through what's here. I'll call the police."

She walked toward the dresser, groaning. "Just what I need. Another night getting an intimate view of police procedurals. Mrs. Drago's going to be upset about this."

He agreed. "I feel bad for her, but it happens in the hotel business."

By the time he got through to Mrs. Drago and to the police, Leslie had gone through her things.

"Nothing's missing," she said, looking stronger and more like herself.

"Nothing?" he repeated in disbelief.

"Nothing. Granted, I don't have much, but my diamond stud earrings would be worth something to a burglar. And they're in full view in my jewelry bag."

"Maybe he thought they were glass."

"Even if he did, I would think he'd take them on the off chance they weren't."

"True. Maybe he was interrupted, like that time in London." He wondered if the Adams had anything to do with these happenings. *Naaa*, he thought in wry amusement at his imagination.

"I don't think he would have gotten this far if he was. Do you think someone just wanted to trash the room?"

He made a face. "Actually I hope not."

Mrs. Drago rushed in, fussing and beside herself with distress. The police weren't far behind, and from their concern it was obvious this sort of thing rarely happened.

As they went down to the station, Mike couldn't help thinking about obstacles. This one was a doozy. But at least it meant Leslie couldn't make a great escape.

He had an urge to kiss the burglar out of sheer gratitude.

Leslie trudged wearily up the steps of the hotel, feeling a sense of déjà vu. Fortunately it was only three in the morning. The local police only had about twenty forms to be filled out, compared with the Yard.

Mr. Drago had come with them, never saying

a word the entire time. He'd been sent by his fluffy and formidable wife to "look out for these poor little lambs," and he'd done exactly that. Just looked out.

"We're actually getting in at a decent hour," Mike said as they waited for Mr. Drago to open up the front doors.

She couldn't help chuckling. "I was thinking the same thing."

Inside, Mr. Drago left them with a wave of his hand. They trudged up the stairs under the dim night-light. Leslie sighed, exhausted. "I don't know whether to be happy or not that no one else in the hotel got hit. Do I have a magnet attached to me that draws English burglars? I've never been robbed at home, although Lord knows what I'll find there now."

"People have the funny idea that all Americans are fat cats," Mike said. "You're an American, ergo you're a fat cat with lots of goodies worth stealing."

"Would you put the word out that I'm a skinny dog with two pairs of socks and a borrowed hair dryer?"

He patted her back. "A gorgeous skinny dog with two pairs of socks and a borrowed hair dryer, but okay."

She could feel the guard around her emotions dissolving at his touch. It didn't matter that it was only meant to be comforting. Mike's warmth was touching her, warming her. He'd been wonderful again that night, patient and kind, supportive of her at every turn. After her firm rejection another man would have left her to her own devices. Not Mike. It was as if she couldn't dent him . . . and she didn't want to. That scared her most of all.

As they walked down the silent corridor, Leslie could feel her resolve sloughing away, leaving her vulnerable. She wanted him. She might have been embarrassed and shocked at herself this morning, but she still wanted him. One look at him and her body went into delicious aftershocks. And getting closer and closer to her doorway only reinforced her feelings.

"I'm not sure I like you here tonight," Mike said in a low voice when they reached her room.

It sounded like a line, and that stiffened her resolve again. "And where would you have me be?"

"Now, don't go crazy on me." He grinned. "I was about to suggest that we could switch rooms if you were uncomfortable."

"I won't be uncomfortable," she said confidently. Common sense told her that the perpetrator was long gone by now. And if he wasn't, he would probably be too scared to do anything again after all the fuss. Her room was probably the safest one in all England tonight.

He took her key from her hand and opened the door. "I'll check it first. You wait here."

She didn't protest, grateful, in a cowardly way, for the manly gesture.

He emerged, handing back her key. "Okay."

"Thanks. Thanks for everything."

But as she walked over the threshold, a wave of illogical anxiety swept over her. "Mike, I think I'll take you up on your offer."

He smiled at her. "I don't blame you."

"Are you sure you'll be all right?"

"I think I can manage. Stop worrying. I'll be fine. Or rather, don't stop worrying, but I'll be fine."

Something in her expression must have given her away, she thought. She'd have to be more careful about that for the time she was still around him. Somehow that thought hurt most of all. She ducked her head. "I'll go get some things."

"Fine."

He waited at the doorway while she gathered nightgown, robe, and morning essentials. She slipped past him into the corridor again, half embarrassed by her vulnerability on the fear scale. He escorted her to his room, unlocked the door, and handed over the key.

"Remember, I'm just down the hall. Call me if you're nervous. I'll even hear a healthy scream."

She smiled at him. "Thanks, Mike. This whole vacation would have been a disaster if it wasn't for you."

He grinned. "I've been wanting to hear that."

Her gratitude turned swiftly to something much more powerful. Leslie gazed up at him, her thoughts swirling in confusion. Her determination to keep him at bay seemed so silly. What was she fighting but her own wants and needs? Why was she so scared to take chances? What did it matter if she was a vacation fling? Wouldn't he be the same? And what if he and she were something more? She'd never know if she didn't throw all caution to the winds. Maybe Gerry had the right idea about relationships after all.

And one thing she did know was that she didn't want to sleep alone tonight.

She reached up and kissed him, wrapping her arms around his neck, trapping half her things between them while the others dropped with a thump on the rug. His aroma invaded her senses, imprinting itself on her forever. She could feel his heat, latent and waiting, as she took him by surprise. His mouth was warm and opening, allowing her access, mating his tongue to hers. His arms came around her, his hands splaying across her back, holding her tightly. She clung to him. The way his hard body aligned itself so perfectly to hers was almost too much. She pressed closer, wanting more, needing more. And she would have more . . . in his bed tonight.

Mike eased his mouth away, gently pulling her arms from around his neck. "No, Leslie. We need to stop now, before we can't stop at all."

"But . . ."

"When you're ready. Damn, but I can't believe I'm doing this."

He kissed her on the cheek, a fleeting warmth, a touch of promise of all he could create inside her, then he was gone, walking back down the corridor.

Leslie walked into the room, numbed by his wisdom and his rejection. She'd thrown herself at him, and she didn't know whether to be furious or grateful that he'd kept his senses.

She changed and crawled into bed, grateful at least for the refuge he'd offered. Slowly, however, she recognized the biggest danger she hadn't foreseen. She was in Mike's bed, pressing her face into Mike's pillow, stretching her body along the same mattress as he'd stretched his. The knowledge pervaded her senses, causing her blood to slow and throb through her veins. The faint scent of him was still on the pillowcase. Images of what they could be doing right then filled her mind. His absence filled her soul with need. All the common sense cautions didn't seem to matter against this.

She wouldn't sleep at all that night, she thought in despair.

And she didn't.

Despite tons of makeup the next morning, Leslie was sure Mike could easily see the signs of her restless night. If he did, he didn't let it show.

"It was a quiet night," he said as he let her

into her room. "I cursed myself for it. How did you sleep?"

"Fine," she lied.

"You would," he muttered.

She allowed herself a brief private smile. It was nice to know he suffered too.

"So what are we doing today?" he asked.

She frowned. "I don't know."

"We could drive down and see Penzance, Land's End, and Saint Michael's Mont. That's a monastery on an island that you can only reach by foot when the tide's out."

"I thought that was in France," she said, careful not to get too close to him as she put things away.

"There is. And one here."

The telephone rang before she could answer. She rushed to it, saying, "Maybe it's the police with information."

Even if she hadn't had anything stolen, it would still feel good to know the culprit was behind bars.

But it was only Gerry on the line.

"Let me guess," Leslie said. "You're not coming to Shrewsbury either."

"I can't leave him," Gerry said, her voice shaking. "I love him. Please, please understand."

Leslie sighed. "Even though I'll kill you when I see you, I do understand."

"Oh, God, no one has ever had a friend like you. You're wonderful."

"And you forgot to pack the hair dryer," Leslie said, making a face at Mike, who grinned back.

"No, I didn't," Gerry replied. "I made sure it was packed, because I knew you'd kill me if I didn't."

"You must have forgotten, because it's not here."

"That's impossible."

Leslie frowned. "Well, never mind. Listen, what the heck are you doing carting around a valuable book like the Adams? Are you crazy? You could ruin it—"

"What book? What Adams?"

"*Pamela. Virtue Rewarded.* By Samuel Richardson. It's a first-edition copy that was given to Abigail Adams by her husband, John. Didn't you read the flyleaf? Where did you get it anyway?"

"What the heck are you talking about? The only book I brought was Johanna Lindsey's latest, and I stuffed that in my purse when we landed. Don't you remember me reading it?"

Leslie *did* remember Gerry sitting next to her at takeoff with her nose in the paperback book so that she wouldn't get nervous. It definitely hadn't been the Adams.

"But I don't understand . . . hold on." She set the receiver down and went over to the luggage, grabbing up Gerry's blue carry-on.

"What?" Mike asked.

"I don't know." She dumped the contents

onto the bed, then picked up the receiver. "Gerry?"

"Is that a man with you?" Gerry asked. "I heard a man's voice there. Did you meet *him*? Is that why you're not upset with me?"

Leslie set her teeth together for a long moment, then said, "Listen up. This is important. What brand of toothpaste did you bring?"

"Aim."

The toothpaste tube was Crest.

"What color comb?"

"I only brought a brush. What is this about?"

"I'll tell you later. What kind of deodorant did you bring?"

"Roll-on."

The deodorant on her bed was a spray.

"What else was in your carry-on?"

"My makeup, a nightie, a change of underwear, and my sinus pills. I found some great stuff here for that, by the way. . . ."

None of those things had been in the carry-on.

"I think you somehow got the wrong carry-on," Leslie said, eyeing Mike. He raised his eyebrows at her. "Thanks, Gerry. I'm leaving for Shrewsbury tomorrow. Hopefully I'll see you on the plane."

She hung up. "The Adams isn't hers."

"That explains a lot," Mike said.

EIGHT

"What do you mean, 'That explains a lot'?"

Mike grinned at Leslie. "Sweetheart, think about it for a moment and your common sense will tell you that two burglaries at opposite ends of a country are a little too much of a coincidence—"

"It could happen."

"One in a million. Maybe. I wondered about it, then passed it by. But now that we know the book isn't Gerry's, the odds are that someone's trying to get back the valuable book that went off with the wrong person."

"But why don't they just ask? Why try to steal it?"

"Maybe because they can't ask—"

"Because they stole it in the first place," Leslie finished excitedly. "And to think I read mysteries all the time. How could I have missed it?"

"Because this isn't Sherlock Holmes. This is real life."

"Wait a minute," she said, common sense finally coming to the fore. "It's really far-fetched to think what's happened to me had anything to do with Gerry's bag mix-up. More than likely there's some legitimate collector frantic because he's got Gerry's five-ninety-nine paperback in a bag that doesn't belong to him while his rare volume has vanished with some ditz, namely Gerry. Lucky for him I got it instead. Gerry probably would have read the thing while taking a bubble bath."

Mike shuddered at the thought of all that moisture and soap working their molecular way into the fragile book materials. And if the imaginary Gerry accidentally dropped the Adams into the imaginary tub . . . "God, I don't even want to think about it. The Adams is a treasure, it should be treated like a queen."

"You know, you are going overboard about a book."

Somehow the way her lips had thinned told him she was annoyed on several levels. He raised his brows. "Are you jealous about a book?"

"Don't be silly. And anyway, we were talking about the book just being lost in a mix-up, not stolen."

"You were the one who brought up my going overboard."

"You were the one practically swooning."

He grinned. "You *are* jealous!"

"Don't be ridicu—"

He cut off her last word with a resounding kiss. The feel of her body, soft and instinctively inviting in his arms, was intoxicating. He kissed her again, slower, savoring the taste of her lips on his, loving the way her hands clutched at his biceps, the nails digging in slightly.

"Just keep on being jealous," he murmured when he lifted his head.

"Don't bet on it," she murmured back, leaning against him but not giving an inch to him mentally.

He just grinned and let her go. "You were saying . . ."

She took a deep breath. "I was saying that we're jumping to conclusions about the book . . . in a lot of ways."

"Whatever way we're thinking, we'd better go get the Adams and see the police."

Leslie groaned. "Not again. Please, not again."

He laughed. He couldn't blame her. "If wishes were horses . . ."

"Yes, yes, another quote. Here's one: To err is human, to not go back to that damn police station is divine." Leslie sighed. "I'm coming."

Once they were in the corridor, he put his arm around her, pulling her body close to his as they walked together. He expected her to pull away, but she didn't. It was as if she had already surrendered physically to him. Not mentally, not emotionally. That would take much longer. Maybe she just didn't want him thinking she was jealous of a book.

He smiled to himself, knowing that had stung her. He wanted to touch her, needed to touch her after last night. He had been stupid to walk away from her then. Now, having her against him, her scent teasing his awareness, only made him realize how much he truly wanted her.

"I was a fool last night," he said when they opened the door to his room and he saw the mussed bed. The bed she had slept in . . . alone. "I should have stayed with you. You were nervous. You needed a companion. I was afraid I'd become a lover again when you weren't ready for me. Dammit, I should have stayed!"

"No." She smiled up at him. "You were right not to stay."

He groaned. "You would say that. Just know I want you badly enough to wait."

She turned away, as if suddenly shy. Leslie being shy was rather like fairies suddenly turning into seven-foot giants. It just didn't happen. But here she was, almost blushing. A man could live for days on this kind of thing, he happily decided.

They retrieved the Adams and went to the police station. There was initial confusion by the police over people trying to return missing goods that none of them was aware had been missing. Mike and Leslie were finally ushered into a tiny, cramped cubicle of an office, and the burly good-natured sergeant they'd been dealing with made a few phone calls.

He hung up the telephone finally and announced, "We'll have to detain you as witnesses until someone from the Yard gets here to begin further investigation."

"But why?" Leslie asked before Mike could.

The sergeant scowled at them. "It seems the book was stolen."

"But she didn't steal it!" Mike exclaimed, realizing Leslie was under suspicion of the theft. "She found it."

"The commander from the Yard will determine that."

"Can't we go back to the hotel and wait?" Leslie asked hopefully. "I promise we won't go anywhere."

"Sorry, miss."

Mike bounded to his feet. "This is ridiculous! Why the hell would she turn in the book if she was the one who stole it? It doesn't make sense."

"Maybe not. But I was told to hold her under suspicion until the Yard got here."

"Anybody know a good English lawyer?" Leslie asked, tears welling up in her eyes.

Mike sat down in his chair again and put his arms around her, pulling her against him. "Honey, it'll be okay. I promise."

She sniffled. "I may hold you to it."

He stroked her hair. "Do that."

"I'm sorry, miss," the sergeant said with professional sympathy. "You too, sir."

"Me too?" Mike gaped at him. "You mean I'm under arrest too?"

"Detained, sir, like the lady here."

"But I only met her in London!"

"Thanks for standing by your woman, Mike," Leslie said in disgust, struggling out of his embrace.

He grabbed her and pulled her back to him. "I'm standing as close as I can get. I was just a little shocked. A lot shocked."

"They do this in America, don't they?" the sergeant asked, frowning in puzzlement. "I see it on the telly all the time when the shows come over."

"Not quite," Mike said. "Unless you're under arrest, you get to go home after questioning. In the States you're innocent until proven guilty. Here I believe you're guilty until proven innocent, right?"

The sergeant nodded. "Pretty much. We like to think that's why the crime rate here isn't off the beam like you people have."

Leslie shivered. "For all its flaws, I think I like our system better. What do we do now? Go to our cells and wait for this guy?"

"Could we have adjoining cells, please?" Mike asked. "Preferably alone."

The sergeant laughed. "No. You can sit here

in this office. Would you like a cuppa? Tea? Coffee?"

"Tea for both of us," Mike said.

When the sergeant left, Mike tightened his hold on Leslie. "It'll be all right."

Leslie buried her face in his shirtfront for a long moment, accepting the comfort, before saying, "I wonder if criminals get one phone call in England. And who would we call, if we did?"

"The American embassy," Mike said promptly.

"Oh, so you've been in this sort of mess before?"

"Like the sergeant said: It's what they do on the telly all the time. That's good enough for me." He drew in a deep breath. "Since we're stuck here waiting, let's talk about us. I hope my getting arrested with you proves how I feel."

She gave a shaky laugh. "I think you're wonderful."

He kissed her. "I needed to hear that too. If we ever get out of this, I'm coming with you to Shrewsbury. No argument."

"None given." She sighed. "Somehow I think walking in the footsteps of a fictional detective will pale in comparison to this."

"Ah, but Shrewsbury is delightful." Wanting to cheer her up, he quoted, " 'High the vanes of Shrewsbury gleam; Islanded in the Severn stream . . .' "

"Mike, one more Housman quotation by jail light and I'll stuff your tie down your throat."

"Well put, love."

He kissed her hair as they settled in to wait.

The Yard detective, a small man who looked like a nervous ferret, took several hours to arrive, but when he did, he was more thorough in his questioning than their last Yard experience. One thing he did allow was a call to the embassy, which promised vaguely to help. Finally, his nose twitching in distaste, he said, "I'm not happy that you don't have your . . . *friend's* address or telephone number, very coincidental that, but she has been confirmed as being on the plane with you—"

"I told you," Leslie said in exasperation, "that she picked up the wrong carry-on!"

"And didn't notice?" The Yard man raised his eyebrows in clear disbelief. "How could anyone not notice they didn't have their own bag?"

"If you knew my friend, you'd know that is practically a given!"

She hadn't cried, and Mike was proud of her for that, but he could see now that she was losing her control. He stepped in. "Officer, if you checked with the airlines, I'm sure you'll find that people pick up the wrong bags quite often because of popular models. That isn't unusual at all. You're holding this woman wrongly—"

"She's a witness," the man snapped. "And I find your story a bit bizarre too. I'm wondering if you've been hanging around to get this Adams book."

"Me!" Mike gaped at him.

"Yes, you. You know all about the book. You pick her up as soon as she gets here, you come down here to Cornwall with her on a lark. You say you're smitten." He glanced at Leslie and sniffed with clear disbelief. "None of it holds up."

Mike rose to his feet, towering over the little ferret. "Leslie is a beautiful woman, you lowlife, and anyone would be smitten. She was in trouble because her friend up and left her, and I helped her out. Just because you think chivalry is dead doesn't mean every man does! I told you to go check with Cambridge University, and with Temple University in the States. They'll confirm me."

"Next you'll be trying to tell me you're in love," the Yard man said, glaring up at him.

"Maybe I am. Dammit, we brought the book in! We didn't know it was stolen! Well, I thought maybe it might be, but why would we try to return it if we were involved in stealing it? Even if things were hot for us, as you claim, then why wouldn't we just mail it to you anonymously?"

"Sit down, man," the detective said, actually giving him a smile. "That's a point I can't get past either. Not yet."

Mike sat, fuming mad at the twerp. *Give a clown a badge and he runs away with authority*, he thought. Why weren't countries training their police staff better and weeding out the blowhards? It mystified him completely.

He realized Leslie was staring at him, openmouthed.

"What?" he asked, although his concentration was on trying to find a way out of this mess they were in.

"Do you . . ." She hesitated. "Do you mean it? About maybe being in love."

Mike blinked in confusion, then remembered what he'd said. He swallowed, everything coalescing inside him. Love at first sight made a helluva lot of sense. "I think so. How do you feel about it?"

"I don't know." She looked ready to cry again.

"Good. Keep that thought." He'd take anything in the way of acceptance right now, but he turned to the more immediate problem. "Look, Leslie is exhausted and you've been over this twenty times. The answer's still the same. She's a time management consultant, and I'm a professor of literature. We're returning a valuable book we found, and beyond that we haven't a clue! Send us back to the hotel, let us both get some rest, and we promise not to make a move without letting you know first. Hell, stake us out! We welcome it."

The ferret-man stared at him, clearly measuring things in his mind. Mike resisted the urge to smash the man's face in, having a feeling that wouldn't help their cause.

"As I was about to say before, while I'm not happy about not having Miss Kloslosky's friend's current address and telephone number, I will allow you to go on with your holiday, as long as we can reach you at all times."

Leslie jumped up and threw her arms around the ferret-man, thanking him profusely. His jaw dropping, Mike stared at her, not believing that *he* wasn't getting the hugs.

"Please, miss, please!" the Yard man protested, his face beet red.

Leslie let him go. "I can't thank you enough, sir. This has been a nightmare."

"Yes. Yes." The man smoothed his mussed hair. Mike's jaw was still on the ground.

Somehow he managed to walk out of the room with her, even out of the station. Then he finally found his voice. "That idiot puts us through hell and you hug him! I talk my backside off and you hug him!"

"I'm sorry," she said . . . and threw herself at him.

Her body hit his solidly, wonderfully. He put his arms around her, feeling every inch of her against him. "That's better."

She buried her face in his neck. "I'll say. He was way too short."

Mike laughed. "God, Leslie, let's go home."

Home was the hotel, with Mrs. Drago mortified at what had happened and fussing over them again. She hustled Leslie off to her room with a hot toddy, leaving Mike trailing wistfully behind.

When he was in his own lonely room, he muttered, "Well, you're in it now."

He'd admitted the truth and put his emotions on the line. Never had he felt so vulnerable. He wished he knew how Leslie felt in return. Being on the fence was hell.

He was too keyed up to sleep, so he stripped off his clothes and put on pajama bottoms, then began the quick, rhythmic movements of Gijianelbo, the first basic form of movement. He went straight through his forms, then began all over again.

When he finally flopped on the bed, he was physically tired, but knew sleep would still elude him. *So much for being a Good Samaritan*, he thought.

Life was hell.

Leslie moaned and put her hands to her temples, trying to keep her head from spinning off her body.

What a mess, she thought, as she tossed restlessly in her bed. Mike's announcement that he might love her scared her, yet she wanted to reach out and grab at it too. She wasn't a person who fell in love at first sight, let alone have someone feel that way about her. Their current situation was exciting, beyond exciting, but he'd find out how dull she really was eventually. Just because she was under suspicion of grand theft didn't mean she'd changed inside.

Leslie groaned at the thought of the trouble she was in. They could come and arrest her at any moment. Being jailed in a foreign country would be horrifying, but that seemed so far away compared with what Mike had said.

Maybe all this excitement was the only reason he thought he was in love with her. She moaned and turned the other way, the notion eating at her heart. But he did only *think* it, after all. She didn't want to grab at it, only to find it slipping through her fingers in the end. Maybe she only wanted it because she was over thirty and *he* was exciting.

She didn't want to make a mistake. Common-sense Leslie Kloslosky didn't make mistakes about love.

She tossed and turned some more, not finding any spot comfortable. She knew she should be exhausted, but thoughts kept flying through her head, keeping her awake. She pushed covers around, scrunched pillows over and over until she couldn't stand it any longer.

She got up, put on her robe, took her room key, then peeked out her door. Seeing no one in the hall, she scooted to Mike's room and knocked softly. The moment she did, all her common sense came back to the fore, and she nearly turned to leave when the door didn't open instantly. But another, more overwhelming urge surfaced. She knocked again.

Mike opened the door a crack, his naked shoulders visible in the light behind him.

"I need to be held," she said, every inch of her skin crying out for the touch of another's.

He opened the door wider, and she slipped through, directly into his arms. He was wearing pajama bottoms, and his flesh was warm, almost hot, his chest hair like a silken mat against her cheek. She curled her fingers into it, taking pleasure in the way it tickled her palms. His scent, already so imprinted on her senses, filled them reassuringly. His hands rubbed her back, circling in almost a massage. She could feel her muscles relaxing. He was strong and real, and she was here with him.

"This could be dangerous," he said.

"I don't care. I couldn't stand my room. I don't want to be alone when they come to arrest me."

He chuckled. "They're not going to arrest you. They would have done it already if they were."

"But why didn't they?" she asked, nuzzling his chest. Lord, but she loved doing that, loved being short enough with this man *to* do it. "We had the book, so I would have thought we'd be detained longer at the least."

"I don't know why, but I'm damned grateful for it." She could feel him turning his head to look at something in the room. "It's not too late in the States. I could give my friend a call and see if he knows how the Adams was stolen. Maybe if we know that, we'll know the 'why,' and whether we're going to be out of trouble. Or in worse."

She nodded. "You were right, you know, about the Adams being stolen. You're making a lot of sense."

He chuckled. "There's a scary thought. Here, why don't you lie down while I make the call."

After a moment's hesitation she obediently went with him to the bed, allowing him to tuck her under the covers. Just like last night, his scent pervaded the sheets, but this time it was comforting. She knew what would happen and she didn't care. He had said he thought he loved her, and she couldn't walk away from that. Sometimes the impulsive meant emotional survival.

She snuggled down into the sheets, feeling all the tensions drain out of her. Mike sat on the side of the bed, the mattress sagging with his weight. His back was to her as he dialed, and she smiled to herself, admiring his muscles, not heavy but compact, yet discernible under his skin. She resisted the urge to reach out and caress him, wanting to savor the view for as long as possible. She liked him, she acknowledged. The rest of her emotions were in a state of deadlocked confusion, but she truly liked him.

"Hello, Jim?" he said into the receiver, clearly getting an answer to his call. "No, I haven't seen the Jonson script yet. . . . I'm not in Cambridge . . . something else came up. . . ."

I'll say, Leslie thought, and grinned. Not only was she becoming impulsive, but she was getting a dirty mind too.

". . . I'm sorry to call so late, Jim, but what do you know about that first-edition copy of Richardson's *Pamela*, the Adams, being stolen?"

A lassitude crept into Leslie's veins, and she closed her eyes, content just listening to Mike's voice, the deep timbre of it thrumming inside her, making her feel protected. Coddled. Everyone needed to be coddled once in a while. She needed it now.

". . . I see. . . . Actually I'm with someone who found it . . . yes, yes . . . Jim, it's beautiful, truly beautiful . . . excellent condition. . . . I had it in my hands. . . ."

Mike's voice went on and on, waxing enthusiastic with another connoisseur of the printed word. The sounds were soothing to her, so soothing that she found she didn't have the energy to open her eyes again. Eventually the sounds faded and a darkness built of trust, warmth, and security closed around her. She fell asleep.

". . . it's a long story," Mike said, realizing he'd been on the phone quite a while. Leslie was lying in his bed, and he was wasting time. "I've told most of it anyway, Jim."

"You really had it in your hands?" Jim's voice was excited as he asked the question for the tenth time. He had known nothing about the theft.

"Saw Adams's John Hancock and everything." Mike grinned. "Wouldn't that be a helluva shock if the dedication *was* from Hancock?"

Jim laughed. "It would be more like *Adultery Rewarded*, and more than priceless, if one could conceive of it."

Mike said, "Look, let me know if you hear anything, okay? Here's the number where I am." He recited it off the phone base. "I expect we'll stay on another day or so, then we're supposed to move to Shrewsbury—"

"That's Brother Alaric country."

"So I'm learning." Mike smiled wryly. He really would have to read the books now. Even Jim, head of the English Department and expert in Federalist literature, was a fan of Leslie's fictional detective. "I'll call you from there, just to check."

He hung up the phone and turned around. Leslie was sound asleep, her hands tucked under her cheek. Mike stared for a few moments, cursed the fates that he knew were right, then turned out the lights. He walked around the bed and slipped in beside her, deciding that if her back were to him, the torture would be less severe. He knew he was wrong as he stretched out his length along hers and put his arm around her waist, tucking her into him. He could feel her back against his chest and her derriere nestled to the most intimate part of himself. His thighs braced hers. She never moved. Life was definitely hell.

Delicious hell.

NINE

Leslie slowly opened her eyes, already aware of the heavy weight against her back. She was in bed with Mike.

Immediate panic at what to do left her in a state of frozen confusion. She couldn't move. She couldn't think. She just lay there.

Taking a deep breath, she admitted her current position didn't surprise her. She'd felt so alone and vulnerable last night, so scared at not knowing what would happen with the police. She'd needed another human being who understood, who could stand with her, and that was Mike. But he also was seducing her in unexpected ways, until she needed his touch overwhelmingly. Even now, with her robe still cinched around her waist, she knew nothing more intimate than sleep had happened between them. And that was even more endearing, when she considered how vulnerable she'd been last night.

Maybe he didn't want her.

That thought galvanized her. Her face heated, and her brain and body clicked on. If he didn't want her—and it was a distinct possibility, since he hadn't attempted to make love—then the last place she wanted to be was in his bed. And she especially didn't want him to find her with her hair all mussed, chenille marks on her cheek, and bad breath. Then he *really* wouldn't want her. She glanced at his travel alarm clock, filing away vague surprise that he actually used one. It was just after seven in the morning. She slowly pushed his arm away, trying not to wake him as she got up and out.

"Relax," he suddenly said in amusement from behind her, his arm tightening back into place. "You're safe with me . . . unfortunately."

She became aware of a hard bar pressing against the small of her back, as if to belie his words. He moved slightly, removing the intimate pressure.

"Okay, so I'm having a little safety trouble," he said, "but I don't want you to get up yet."

She turned her head slightly to look at him. His hair was tousled, making him look boyish, and a slight shadow of a beard ran along his jaw and chin. She didn't give a damn if he had morning breath, she wanted to kiss him so badly. Only the thought of her own held her back. "This isn't such a good idea."

"You're thinking 'common sense' again. You've got to stop that. Why can't a man and a woman just lie down in bed together? It can be done. Millions of old married people do it, though heaven only knows how. . . ."

She found herself chuckling and relaxing, although a little voice told her that if she rolled over and they faced each other, all good intentions would be lost. She turned away from him and settled back on the pillow.

"Let's talk, maybe that will help," he went on.

"We don't know a lot about each other," she admitted.

"We know the most important things," he said, his arm tightening for an instant.

"But we don't know a lot of small things about each other." This was scary, she thought. Another seduction, yet she couldn't resist. "Such as, do you have a pet?"

"An old basset hound named Keats. He'll love you. He loves everybody. What about you? You've got to have a cat. It's so sensible."

She chuckled. "I do. Tobias. But he's very unsensible. I can never seem to get him quite housebroken, and he clawed up the sofa before I got him declawed. But I like him."

"I think I like him too. Keats couldn't claw up anything, even on his good days. He never moves from the easy chair."

"I think I like him."

"What's your favorite color?"

"Blue. Yours?"

"Red."

"What news channel do you watch?

"Channel Three."

"Six. Ice cream?"

"Vanilla."

"Banana."

They weren't matching up much, she thought, then dismissed the negative notion. This was interesting. She asked, "Do you like sports?"

"No."

"Thank goodness."

"Did you have a good childhood?"

"Yes." She smiled. "I'm not maladjusted. Just sensible."

He chuckled. "I had a good childhood, too, but it didn't make me sensible."

"Not all of us are blessed." The sun was shining through the crack in the window curtains. Leslie knew she really ought to go before the morning traffic started in the halls.

"What's your secret dream?" he asked.

She rolled over to face him, frowning. "My secret dream?"

He nodded. "Your secret dream. The one thing you would love to achieve in life. Mine is to be a rock star. Don't laugh."

She giggled anyway, trying to imagine him flinging himself around on a stage. Of all the things he would want to be, she just couldn't conceive of this one.

He made a face. "I can't help it. I was raised on Steppenwolf and Iron Butterfly. So what's your secret dream?"

"I . . . I don't have one."

He raised up on one elbow in surprise. "Don't have one? Leslie, of course you do. Everyone does. They want to be president or Babe Ruth or a movie star or a millionaire. You have to have one of those."

She shook her head, her hair rubbing against the pillow.

He narrowed his gaze. "You're not telling me because you think you'll look silly. I already look silly, and it's not so bad. What is it? It's got to be good. Give."

She shook her head more vehemently, tears starting to fill up behind her eyes. Why should not having a secret dream upset her? But it did. "I don't have one. I never wanted to be anything or get anything. It always seemed so silly to wish for something that was impossible, so I never did."

Now he really knew how dull and boring she truly was.

He stared at her for a moment, mouth gaping, then sighed. "I'm sorry. Everyone should have a secret dream. We'll just have to find you one."

She gazed up at him, believing him somehow. He leaned forward until their lips touched. The kiss was tentative and sweet. His hand was heavy on her, his fingers spread across her stomach, holding her. She reached up and touched his cheek, loving the way his morning whiskers bristled along her palm. The one small touch ignited them both, and the kiss turned passionate. She dug her nails into his shoulders, lifting herself up into his chest. She groaned as her already sensitive nipples grazed his flesh.

He broke off the kiss suddenly and buried his face in her shoulder. "I want you so much. . . . We need to stop now."

"No." She pulled his mouth back to hers.

This time she was taking for herself whatever she could before it was gone. Impulse was buried by overwhelming necessity. Excuses and constraints were nothing against the forces inside her requiring fulfillment—fulfillment only by him.

This time, in a bed, when he took her to the heights and over, again and again, frantically, leisurely, desperately, and assuredly, she knew a certainty deep in her soul that would last forever.

Just as he'd promised, she'd found her secret dream.

"We didn't break the bed."

Leslie laughed. "You sound disappointed."

Mike ran his hand along the side of her breast, down her waist and hip, his fingers curling slightly into her skin, sending the first stirring through her veins. "Nope. We're going to need this bed again." He raised himself up and gazed down at her worriedly. "Are we going to use this bed again?"

"Yes." She smiled at him. "Yes."

He relaxed. "Good."

She should be uncomfortable being naked with him like this, but she wasn't. She knew what she was doing now, she thought, as he turned onto his side, bringing her with him. It wasn't sensible, but she was tired of being sensible. And dull. She didn't expect it to last beyond her vacation, no matter what Mike thought or said, but she would live with that. She knew reality and now she was prepared to accept it. She hadn't been living before, and that's what she needed to do now, to stop going through life sensibly. Life wasn't sensible. Needs weren't sensible. They just were, and couldn't be denied.

"So when are we going to Shrewsbury?" Mike asked.

The last leg of her journey, the part she'd waited for and saved for, now was like a lead weight in her stomach. She didn't want to go, for when she did, that meant her trip was almost over. And her time here with Mike. Whether it would resume in the States, she didn't know, but she refused to expect anything of him, and she wouldn't ask. She took a deep breath and said, "The tour starts the day after tomorrow."

"Good." He grinned. "With us being in trouble with the law now, we ought to fit right in."

She chuckled. "That's true."

Still, she couldn't shake the sense of loss already looming in the back of her mind.

"How long will we be there?" he asked.

"Five days." What she didn't want to say—"And then I go home"—hung in the air between them during the ensuing silence.

"You're not a fling." He kissed her gently, then firmly. "You're not a fling."

"No," she whispered, wanting to trust him.

He seemed satisfied, smiling at her, that she accepted his words. And she really did on one level. She was positive he meant it, but she still couldn't help feeling that all good intentions would disappear the moment they parted. Like two teenagers who met at a summer resort, all that true love always disappeared the moment September came. At seventeen one had resiliency. At thirty-three one had desperation.

Worse, Mike hadn't said again that he thought he loved her.

She drew in a mental deep breath and turned her thoughts aside. Whatever would come, would come. She couldn't stop it. She just had to accept each day and not look ahead.

"What do you think will happen with the book?" she asked. "It seems strange now not to have it."

"I expect they'll hold it as evidence." Mike smiled. "I still can't believe *I* held it in my hands."

"I was actually reading it." She made a face. "Now I don't know how it ends."

"She reforms her dissolute employer and marries him, all through her virtue and moral standards."

She remembered that *Virtue Rewarded* was the book's second title. She hadn't kept hers. Would she now pay for it in the end?

"Still," she said, "I'd love to finish it, even knowing it has a happy ending. I hate not finishing things."

"Me too. We'll see if we can get you a copy." He stroked her hair back off her face. "Hungry?"

She shook her head. She probably ought to be, but she didn't want to get up. She wanted to savor this, to watch the way the muscles of his face worked when he smiled . . . to see his eyes darken almost to sapphire. She wanted to see his lazy, satisfied grin and feel his hands on her. She wanted to trace her hands along his chest, feeling the silky hairs against her palms. That always amazed her, she thought, how soft a man's chest hair was. She wanted to feel the rougher hairs of his legs grazing her thighs, so sensitive now to his touch. And most of all, she wanted to take him intimately into the cradle of her hips. Food wouldn't even begin to satisfy her at the moment.

"You've got a funny look in your eye," he said.

"That's supposed to be a come-hither look," she told him.

"I'm already 'hither.' " He pulled her across

the last few inches to him. "And I intend to be hithered out."

She smiled, and could feel the feminine power behind it. " 'Man does not live by bread alone.' "

" 'And every good boy deserves favor,' " Mike replied.

Leslie sighed happily. "You're a Moody Blues fan too. Thank you, Lord."

"Blues, the Beatles, Hendrix, Jethro Tull, Bread, Robert Palmer." He laughed. "I told you that in my secret dreams I wanted to be a rock star."

She smiled. "At least you want to be my kind of rock star."

"That's what counts."

Flesh against flesh was causing its own distraction for her now. She ran her fingers along his chest. "You know what I would like?"

"What?" His voice had a hitch in it, as if she were already affecting him. She hoped so.

"I would like to make love to a rock star."

"Secret dream?"

She began to spread kisses along his jaw. "I'm learning."

The knock at the door came at a propitious moment.

"Just a minute!" Mike called out, silently cursing at the interruption. He and Leslie had been snuggling in the aftermath, about to tackle some harder questions about their relationship—until this. "Who is it?"

"Mrs. Drago, love. There's a policeman to see you and Miss K. Is she with you?"

Mike stared at Leslie, who stared back in horror, then they scrambled away from each other.

"Ah . . . yes. Just a minute." Mike started hunting around for his clothes.

"Oh, Lord." Leslie moaned, pulling on her nightgown and robe. She tied the sash, yanked up the sheets, then leaped into the room's only chair, taking a prim posture.

Mike threw on his own robe, ran a brush through his hair, then flipped it to Leslie.

She blushed, then started to brush her tousled hair into order. She whispered, "I don't believe this. Caught by the cops. Couldn't they have waited? I hate getting arrested with unwashed teeth."

Mike knew the joke was to cover her frayed nerves. This was *not* how he planned a morning-after. Or was it evening?

"We'll take a time-out with a toothbrush, instead of the obligatory telephone call," he said, gripping the doorknob. He took a deep breath. "Ready or not . . ."

Leslie took a deep breath, then nodded. He whipped open the door.

Mrs. Drago was wringing her hands and glancing at the young, nondescript-looking man next to her. "I'm so sorry . . . this is terrible . . . he absolutely insisted. . . ."

The nondescript man smiled politely. He had a large shopping bag dangling from one hand. "That I did." He took out his I.D. and opened it. "Inspector Detective Lawton. I *am* sorry to disturb you, but I would like to speak with you about the book you found."

Mike glanced at Leslie, who was trying not to look nervous, then stepped back. "Come in."

"I'll just go," Mrs. Drago said, and hurried away. Mike had the distinct feeling she would love to be rid of her two problem guests.

"Miss Kloslosky," Lawton said.

Leslie's face had a rosy hue, but she kept her expression composed as she said hello.

Mike closed the door and went to stand next to Leslie. He knew he towered over the man, but Lawton didn't seem intimidated by that fact unfortunately. Mike put his hand on Leslie's shoulder, saying, "I hope we're not going to have more problems, Inspector."

"No. Actually I came partly to apologize for not being available when your find was reported. The man sent from the Yard didn't know this case, and he was harsher than he needed to be with you, I believe. We know neither of you is involved in the theft."

Mike felt the tension rush out of Leslie, even as he slumped in relief.

"Thank God," she said, smiling up at him.

"It's a gang of thieves we've been following for some time," Lawton explained. "They steal priceless artifacts and use innocent people to carry them, usually through a bag mix-up. They're very clever. They wait until the last minute to make the switch with a similar bag in a departure lounge, which nobody notices in the hubbub, and then have someone waiting on the other end who picks it up right away before anyone realizes what's happened. No one gets hurt. Very simple, very easy, very untraceable. Yours is only the second slipup they've had. The first was an alert person who recognized after takeoff that he had the wrong bag and turned it over to the flight attendant. That's when we first got onto their methods. But they made a huge mistake with yours. Do you know if your friend was bothered with break-ins as you were? The report didn't say."

Leslie shook her head. "She didn't say either. But I don't think so, because I did tell her about the ones we had, and she was upset. She would have told me if something similar had happened to her."

"Well, she may have some, if they've gotten onto her. We know they're frantic because they've missed with you twice, had to trace you down, and they can't find her at all. At least they couldn't as recently as yesterday."

"How do you know this?" Mike asked.

"Inside man," Lawton and Leslie said at the

same time. The policeman raised his eyebrows, as she blushed deeper.

"She's a mystery reader," Mike explained.

"Ah." The detective's brow cleared and he grinned. "That makes sense."

"That's her specialty," Mike told him, grinning back.

"I take it the thieves don't know yet that the book's been turned in?" Leslie asked, clearly trying to steer the conversation away from herself.

"No, and it's going to be a well-kept secret for a time, although it's remote now that they'll press their luck and we'll catch them." He gazed at Mike and her for a moment, then opened the shopping bag and took out a familiar blue carry-on. *The* blue carry-on. "But we'd like for you to use the bag again, to keep it visible, and be on the lookout for anyone who acts suspiciously around you. If you're willing. We will understand completely if you are not. By the way, the book isn't in it."

Mike frowned. "I'm not sure I like this. It could be dangerous."

"The one thing these thieves haven't been is dangerous from a physical standpoint," Lawton said. "If they were, we wouldn't even be asking you. If anyone takes the bag, let it go. All we want is a description of the man on this end. These men have been extremely clever, cutting their losses rather than risk using force when things get desperate. It's as if the ruddy bastards take pride in tweaking everybody's noses. One thing they don't do is overplay the odds with violence."

"If they don't overplay the odds, then wouldn't they have cut their losses already?" Mike asked, pleased with his logic.

"Probably they have. But they could try one last time to get it back."

Leslie reached out and took the bag from Lawton. "We'll be happy to do it."

"No, we won't," Mike said, appalled at her decision. "Remember the last time you were impulsive? We were in a cow pasture on a foggy night."

Leslie glanced up at him, even as her face colored for a third time. "I was impulsive again after that, and you weren't complaining. Besides, this isn't impulsive, Mike. This is a slight calculated risk on our part, to catch the thieves. I understand the inspector's point completely and you, who ought to have a deeper appreciation than most for catching men who steal rare editions, should understand too."

Mike set his jaw and argued the point. For five minutes he argued the point.

Leslie just smiled when he was done. "Relax, Mike, this isn't like the movies. Nothing will happen. I doubt we'll see anything beyond blue-haired old ladies the entire time, but it'll be fun to have the bag on the mystery tour in Shrewsbury." She said to the inspector, "That's where we're going next."

"Ah. You're off to see Brother Alaric?"

"*Everyone* knows him," Mike muttered. Poor old Housman was taking a beating against commercial fiction.

The inspector smiled with satisfaction. "Well, then, I'll leave you to it. But don't worry, sir, the possibility's very remote that they'll even show up. Just a bit of covering all stops for us." He took a small white card out of his inside pocket. "Here's my number at the Yard and at home. Call me right away *if* you do see anything suspicious."

He inclined his head and left the room. The door no sooner shut behind him than Mike rounded on Leslie.

"Are you crazy?" he demanded.

She grinned. "Relax. Nothing will happen. And if it does, at the worst somebody will snatch the bag and maybe we'll witness it and can give a positive I.D."

"That's all that had better happen," Mike said, giving in against all instinct. He cursed outright, then said, "You're scary sometimes."

"Thank you."

Mike moaned. She was positively terrifying.

TEN

"See? Blue-haired old ladies."

Leslie grinned in triumph as she glanced around the lobby of the Abbots Mead Hotel. The five people present, other than themselves, looked purposeful and innocent. She had done the driving from Falmouth to Shrewsbury on the M road, a major highway that rivaled any interstate back home. That only added to her smugness.

"*One* blue-haired old lady," Mike said, snorting. "But she does look tame, I'll admit. So does everyone else."

"I do wish the hotel looked more medieval than Georgian," she said. "But it's lovely, really."

The facade, dating back only two hundred years, was light and airy, with large windows and beautiful marble support columns. When she and Gerry had booked there, the Abbotts Mead had sounded like something out of Sir Walter Scott, just what she had been wanting for this part of their trip. But she'd "suffer." This was great suffering.

"I just hope we can change your room from two single beds to a double," he said.

"We can always push the beds together," she reminded him. She was going to enjoy this last fling wholeheartedly, without sense, without reservation.

He kissed her temple. "You're always so wonderfully sensible. Except for that."

He looked pointedly at the infamous blue bag she was holding. Leslie just smiled and made a show of thrusting out the thing into even plainer view. Mike practically growled at her to stop.

"Relax," she said. "Blue-haired old ladies, remember?"

They checked in, managing to get her room changed to more accommodating accommodations. When they got upstairs, Mike closed the door of their room behind them. This time he was smiling.

"Now, this is more like it," he said, coming toward her with a leer on his face.

She raised her eyebrows. "You look like a giraffe who's been at sea too long."

He pulled her to him. "Thank you very much. That was my sexiest look."

There had been a time when she would have sworn that the first thing she would do in Shrewsbury was go out and explore the town, to walk in the fictional footsteps of her favorite character. Instead she smiled and ran her hands up Mike's arms, loving the feel of strength in his biceps and knowing where her heart really was. "We'll work on it."

Later, much later, as they went downstairs for dinner hand in hand, she felt as if the old Leslie, the sensible Leslie, had slipped away forever. She didn't want her back, she admitted. She had to chuckle to herself and also admit that Gerry's premonition about the trip had been right on target. Mike was impulsive enough to fall in love at first sight—*maybe* love at first sight—but she was catching up now. The "maybe love" bothered her, but she couldn't blame him for being unsure. Who could really be sure about another person?

She scolded herself, knowing both of them needed to take things one day at a time. Right now she was with a man who was occupying her thoughts and her body, and she was on the lookout for criminals. What more could a girl ask for? She would tell him tonight how much she had come to care for him, how much he meant to her—how maybe she was already in love. When they got home and all the excitement had died, when they were in their real lives as their real selves, then there could be talk of being sure, because they would know for sure. But tonight, tonight she would make as special as she possibly could.

"Ah," Mike said, stopping them at a little door in the middle of the corridor. "An elevator. I was minding my own business in that elevator back in London, and then you walked in." He kissed her.

Leslie smiled. "I think I love elevators."

He pressed the Down button. A whoosh and a thunk was heard, then the door opened to reveal several people already on.

"But not this one," Leslie said, although she quickly looked at each person, trying to decide if he or she could be their "bag" man.

"Right." Mike waved off the people. "We'll walk down."

The staircase wasn't as grand as in London, but it was wide enough for two and had highly polished wooden steps.

"When do you come home from your sabbatical?" she asked, broaching a subject that had been bothering her.

Mike let go of her hand and put his arm around her, his fingers rubbing her from shoulder blade to waist. "Three months."

She froze. "Three months!"

He nodded, pulling her to him. "I really will feel like a giraffe too long at sea. Promise you'll wait for me."

"You're no Housman," she whispered into his shirt, fighting the sudden urge to cry. Three months!

"This isn't going to die here," he said. "Have faith in me, Leslie."

"I'm still working on 'impulsive.'" She lifted

her head and looked up at him. "I'm tall, plain, and sensible. Everything a man could *not* want."

"You're gorgeous and exciting and everything I *need*." He kissed her, his lips and tongue trying to convey all the promise of his words.

"It's so lovely to see young love," said a chirping voice from above them.

Leslie turned with Mike to find the one blue-haired old lady they'd spotted in the lobby standing on the steps above them. She was smiling with genuine pleasure, not at all affronted by their display of affection.

"We're in your way. I'm sorry," Leslie said. She and Mike began to descend the stairs again.

"Nonsense. I was sorry to have to interrupt you. I'm Mrs. Wilkens. Mary Wilkens."

"Mike Smith and Leslie Kloslosky," Mike said over his shoulder.

"My, but you're a tall one, aren't you? Both of you. Americans just seem to be grander all the way around."

Leslie grinned. They reached the bottom of the stairs and shook hands. Mrs. Wilkens was short, slightly plump, with iron blue-gray hair permed in badly cut short curls that looked incongruous with her round, wrinkled face. She wore a green-flowered dress of silky material, which was far too fragile for her heavy form and was belted firmly at the waist. Her eyeglass frames were straight out of the fifties, curving into points at the temples. Yet her smile was delightful in its infectious charm.

"Are you here for the mystery tour, Mrs. Wilkens?" Leslie asked.

"Oh, yes, I'm doing the tour. I love a good whodunnit," Mrs. Wilkens said.

Leslie coughed politely. "I think this is a 'follow in Brother Alaric's footsteps' kind of tour. There isn't a mystery being acted out."

Except their own.

"Of course." Mrs. Wilkens laughed. "I get so muddleheaded sometimes. Well, I won't keep you young people." She winked. "I'm sure you're heading out to some posh restaurant for dinner . . . or taking a stroll down lovers' lane."

Leslie laughed. "Actually we're going to find a map of the town."

"Dear, dear," she said, frowning. "Young man, you must take your lady to some romantic spot. I insist."

Mike smiled at her. "Yes, ma'am."

"Good. That's settled. And I'll leave you two to it." She said good-bye and retreated down the back of the hotel lobby toward the dining room.

When she was out of earshot, Mike said, "She was cute. Well, sweet is more like it."

Leslie chuckled. "You have to give her credit. Her style is unique. But I think we can count her out of the suspicious-character list."

"Agreed. Anyway our burglar in London was definitely taller, slimmer, and *male.*"

"I can't see her getting past Mrs. Drago without stopping to gossip."

They got their map, along with several brochures, and went out. The sky was that wonderfully velvet gray of late evening, the English summer stretching the days longer than they were used to in Pennsylvania. Mike walked her across English Bridge and the Abbey Foregate, the Severn River moving like a swift, dark band beneath, shot through with silvery lights. The dark silhouette of the abbey itself, setting for the mystery books, rose up above them, swallowing them up in its shadows.

Leslie sighed, deeply satisfied. "Where are we going? Not that I care."

"I'm taking Mrs. Wilkens's advice," Mike said, "and taking you for a romantic stroll in the moonlight."

Leslie's stomach growled. "I think I want the posh restaurant instead."

"Party pooper." But he steered them toward the first restaurant he saw.

As they strolled back into the hotel much later, Leslie said, "I think I must have looked at each man in that restaurant a dozen times, trying to figure out if he was actually the one."

"Mmm." Mike nodded, looking around the lobby area himself.

She nudged him. "You're as bad as me."

"I suppose. I think I would have liked to have

gone through this as an innocent." He reached up and stroked back her hair. "Let's go to bed."

She smiled. "I can think of nothing better. I just hope our room hasn't been ransacked again."

"Bite your tongue." Then he grinned. "Better still, bite mine."

"Race you up the stairs," she challenged.

They were laughing when they arrived at their room, all thoughts of ransacking pushed aside. Mike unlocked the door and opened it. What they saw inside had Leslie's heart plummeting to her feet.

"Leslie!" Gerry O'Hanlon wailed, rushing over and flinging herself into the stunned Leslie's arms. She began to weep copiously.

"How did you get in?" Leslie asked, automatically closing her arms around her friend.

"The manager. Oh, what does it matter." Gerry shook even harder. "Tully doesn't want me anymore!"

"I'd better check the room," Mike said, making a face at Leslie over Gerry's head. "If they let her in, they may have allowed someone else."

Gerry turned, sniffling back tears. "Who's this?"

"Mike Smith," Leslie said, volunteering nothing more. She didn't want to hear anything about premonitions.

Gerry glanced at the double bed, then at Mike, who was opening the closet where the blue bag was, then at Leslie. "You *did* find someone. I told you." Gerry burst into tears again. "Why does this happen to me all the time? I was so positive about Tully. Why wasn't I enough for him?"

Leslie resisted the urge to point out that nobody would be enough for a man who picked up women on airplanes and moved them into his bed. "Did you have any problems, Gerry? Any break-ins or people trying to take your bags?"

That penetrated the weeping. Gerry glanced up, her face red with wet trails down her cheeks and chin. "No. No, why?"

"The bag's here," Mike said, holding up the blue carry-on.

"Oh! You got my bag back—"

"No, this is the one from the switch," Mike said.

"What switch?"

"What switch!" Leslie repeated in astonishment, then realized Gerry didn't know. She explained about the Adams.

Gerry's eyes got wide. "But how could anyone make a switch of my bag without my noticing?"

Leslie was tempted to ask Gerry how she could go off with a man in a foreign country on the spur of the moment, but refrained from doing so. Clearly Gerry was hurting. That was the problem with Gerry, she thought. She loved too freely sometimes. "Who knows," Leslie said, "but it happened."

Gerry's bottom lip trembled. "I was a fool

again, Leslie. And I was horrible to you. I don't know what's wrong with me anymore. Why am I so desperate about men? You have every right to toss me out. But I'm so glad you haven't." She glanced at Mike. "I didn't realize you were with someone. I showed the clerk my reservation confirmation letter and said it must be a mistake when he said you already had a roommate. He thought there was some mix-up, like I did. I mean, I normally would have known about Mike, wouldn't I? And then when I saw his things . . . Well, I didn't know what to do, so I thought I would wait for you."

"It's okay," Leslie said helplessly, patting Gerry on the back.

Gerry sniffled again. "I guess I should get my own room now."

Leslie opened her mouth to agree with her, although she felt truly bad that Gerry was hurting so much and probably needed to talk it out. Mike spoke instead.

"No, Gerry." His voice held resignation. "You stay with Leslie. You had the reservations together. I'll get my own room."

Leslie gaped at him, not even able to find her own voice to protest such a ridiculous idea. He couldn't be serious.

"Oh, no, I couldn't," Gerry said quickly. "That wouldn't be fair to you at all."

"Gerry, there's no discussion," he said. He

opened the door and walked through it before anyone could speak.

"I'm sorry!" Gerry wailed after the door closed behind Mike.

"Excuse me," Leslie said, letting go of her friend and hurrying to the door. She raced down the stairs, not catching him and realizing he must have taken the elevator. He was already at the desk, having the clerk check the registration records when she arrived, puffing for breath.

"You can't!" was all she could get out.

"Leslie, angel," Mike said, smiling sadly. "We would both feel rotten if we threw her out right now. I'm going to hate myself for this, but much as I'd love to say, 'Get yourself another room,' I can't do that."

"I can!" she snapped, finally getting a deep breath in. There was a time when she wouldn't be fighting this, but not now. She couldn't stand not being with Mike. "Gerry's my friend, but—"

"I'm sorry," the clerk said, interrupting her. He was a young man who looked anxious. "We seem to be booked full."

Both of them stared at him, wide-eyed. "You can't be," Mike said.

"You've got to have a room!" Leslie added.

The clerk shook his head. "No, not a one. This is only the second time I've seen this. Good for us, but not so good for you, I'm afraid. I could put a cot in your room. It will cost ten pounds extra a night."

"A cot!" Mike shuddered.

Leslie groaned. The thought of him in the room on a cot was as much torture as the thought of him not there at all. "Can you call another hotel and get a room for Ms. O'Hanlon?"

"Leslie," Mike began.

She glared at him. "No. I feel bad that Gerry's so unhappy, but I will not have her put you out. It's about time she learned to live with her decisions."

"You're being too hard on her," Mike said. "And I'm not going to feel right putting her out."

"Mike!" Leslie's frustration level was nearly to the boiling point. She whirled on the clerk. "You call." She whirled back to Mike. "And you hush up! You're sleeping with me if I have to kill you to do it!"

Mike looked at the ceiling. "How wonderful to know you care."

The clerk didn't press his luck with her, however. He called a number of hotels before reporting, "There aren't any rooms at any of them. Tomorrow begins the Flower Festival, and everyone's booked full."

Leslie moaned, seeing the alternative looming up like Godzilla out of the ocean. "What a mess!"

"I suppose I can do a cot. I'll have to," Mike said. He turned to Leslie. "Don't ever again tell me that you're not exciting. I'm having all the symptoms of a heart attack."

She wrapped her arms around him. "I'll make it up to you, I promise."

"I'll hold you to that."

Gerry, when presented with the new accommodations, absolutely insisted on taking the cot that was squeezed into the room. As soon as it was set up, she lay down on it, refusing to move as if to prove her point.

"If anyone else gets more polite, we'll be a Marx brothers movie," Leslie said, furious at this turn of events. So much for making this a special night. Everything was ruined. Everything.

Getting into pajamas was a farce of a crowded bathroom and tightly sashed robes that were removed only after lights were turned out.

"Good night, Leslie. Good night, Mike," Gerry said.

"Good night, Gerry. Good night, Leslie," Mike said.

"Good night, John-boy," Leslie said in total disgust.

She had finally let go of common sense, and she was stuck with a chaperone for the rest of her trip.

It figured.

Mike lay as far on his side of the bed as he could get. He now knew the real torture of having Leslie in the same bed and not being able to touch her, hold her in his arms, and make love to her.

She moved restlessly, sending ripples out across the mattress to him. He curled his fists to keep himself from responding. The cot would have been better than this. Gerry meant well, he knew that, but she had no idea what kind of torment she was putting him and Leslie through. Other men might be thrilled to have two women in their bedroom, but not him. He thought of the Housman stanza that began, "They hang us now in Shrewsbury jail. The whistles blow forlorn." That could just about sum up this visit to Shrewsbury, because the whistle had been blown on him.

The idea of being in danger over the Adams was so remote now, he couldn't muster more than a modicum of concern for it. He had known this Shrewsbury trip was his last chance to link strong emotional chains with Leslie before they had to separate. That opportunity was gone with Gerry's arrival. He'd like to meet the guy who had dumped Gerry, just to put him in the hospital over what he was doing to Leslie and him.

He had planned to tell her that night, firmly this time, that he loved her—and more. Now there wasn't enough foundation between them, and she might not be waiting for him when he got home. He wished he didn't have to stay on for the Jonson manuscript, but sabbaticals weren't vacations. In academia sabbaticals were commitments to one's lifework and one's job. He had to honor his obligations. If he didn't in this, then how could he prove to Leslie he would honor commitments to her?

When that elevator door in London had opened, he'd known exactly what he wanted for the rest of his life. He just needed time for her to catch up. But time was nearly gone.

Her arm brushed against him as she flipped over, a fleeting touch before she scooted away. Mike's heart thumped hard in his chest, and a thin film of sweat broke out on the back of his neck. He wanted her so badly, he couldn't stand it.

He tried chanting the five creeds of Tang Soo Do, along with visualizing the exercise forms, hoping to relax himself in order to survive the night and think clearly. There was still something left that maybe he could salvage. Maybe.

By the next morning, though, he had nothing—nothing except a night of no sleep and of not touching Leslie once. He still didn't know how he had survived it, although his brain was woolly and his body felt as if he had run an obstacle course ten times.

The three of them went down to breakfast. The morning routine had been an Academy Award performance of modesty by the three of them. Leslie's eyes were red-rimmed and her skin pale. Her expression was set as if in stone. Gerry's expression was hangdog and her eyes were still red too, only in her case from crying. Mike had heard her during the year-long night. He had a feeling that he looked no better.

"Oh, you have another friend."

They turned as a group to find Mrs. Wilkens behind them. She was beaming expectantly. Mike admitted he kind of liked the fluttery old woman, although he was in no mood for her this morning.

"Yes," Leslie said. "My friend, Gerry O'Hanlon. Gerry, this is Mrs. Wilkens. Mike and I met her yesterday."

"Kissing on the steps," Mrs. Wilkens informed Gerry, whose eyes instantly watered. "Oh, dear. Do you have a cold?"

"Yes, she does," Leslie said before Gerry could answer. Mike had a feeling she had staved off a lament on love lost.

"Well, you get some orange juice, child. That helps."

"I'm sorry," Gerry muttered, when the older woman left them.

"It's okay," Mike told her. Leslie, to his surprise, said nothing.

The morning breakfast was for those participating in the tour. Mike got himself signed on, and to his dismay Gerry bravely insisted on going too. He wished she would have stayed at the hotel, giving him and Leslie an opportunity to talk. The guide, a middle-aged woman with an upperclass accent, explained the itinerary of a walking tour of the town, following by dinner and dancing, followed by a second-day bus tour of the suburbs with stops at Alaric book settings, and a third-day finale in Wales before ending up at the abbey itself.

As he looked around the crowded room, he had to admit that no one seemed out of place among the avid mystery readers of Brother Alaric. There were older couples, invariably one eager-looking while the spouse's expression was bored. Several families were present, with the requisite number of fidgety kids. Rounding it out were several single bookish-looking women and men, and a number of blue-haired old ladies, their Mrs. Wilkens among them. All his fears seemed foolish now that they were faced with reality. Whatever men were here looked too soft to be the man who'd raced down several flights of stairs in the blink of an eye. Mike had worried something would happen, and it had—Leslie's friend had shown up. And things were falling apart. Fast.

"If it's any of these, then my grandmother is a hit man for the Mafia," Leslie whispered in his ear.

He grinned at her.

"What?" Gerry asked.

"Nothing," Leslie said.

The woman looked crestfallen, and Mike's heart went out to her. With her red wavy hair and wide-eyed expression, she seemed vulnerable. He didn't know her, but she was trying, he had to admit, and Leslie was all but pushing her away. He'd have to speak to Leslie about that. It wasn't fair for her to take out her anger on Gerry. Still, it was nice to know she *was* angry. That meant she was as disappointed as he. *Strengthening those chains*, he thought with some satisfaction.

Going through the town of Shrewsbury was uneventful. "Islanded in Severn Stream," Housman had called the town, for the Severn River curved around three-quarters of it in a near-perfect moat. The castle sat at the top of the island's hill, its walls burning a fiery orange-red in the bright sunlight. Leslie walked alongside him as the group climbed the streets—"Walking exactly the same path as Brother Alaric does," the guide announced—and he put his arm around her waist, grateful and tortured to be able to touch her even so innocently. All his thoughts were so occupied with her, he belatedly realized Gerry had been walking on the other side of him all the way. He turned to glance at her, but found his gaze caught by something else.

A man, a young man, on the fringes of the tour group, immediately turned his head away from Mike's gaze. He hadn't been with the group at the hotel, Mike was positive of that since he'd looked each person over with a fine-toothed survey. This one had joined them somewhere after the tour had begun. More than that, this newcomer reminded him in height and build of the burglar in London.

Mike turned his gaze forward for a few minutes, then turned quickly back. He caught the young man staring blatantly at them, his mouth dropping at being caught out.

Mike whispered out of the side of his mouth to Leslie, "I think we have a problem."

ELEVEN

"What?" Leslie asked, staring up at him.

Her body thrummed in response before she could control it, a flow of warmth through her belly and thighs. His hand at her waist had only raised her level of awareness, her desire to throw herself into his arms. She had no idea how she was managing to act normal on the outside. Inside she was a raging mass of need. Why had she ever thought she and Mike were incompatible? They were perfectly compatible where it counted. Damn Gerry for showing up when she did.

"I said I think we have a problem."

His mouth was wonderfully mobile, she thought, wondering if anyone would notice if she pulled him into the first doorway they came to and kissed him senseless. And then his tone and expression, far from flirtatious, penetrated. She pulled herself together regretfully. "What problem?"

"A man, a young man, past Gerry, on the fringes of the crowd. He wasn't there before. Could he be our burglar from London? Be careful how you look."

Leslie leaned around Mike, while pointing to a large hanging basket on the far side of the street. "Gerry, isn't that lovely? Back home who would think to mix petunias, lobelia, Wandering Jew, and impatiens together in a hanging basket like that? I could imagine that on your patio."

The young man on the edge of the group immediately looked away from her when she glanced at him.

"You're right," Gerry said, perking up. Leslie had a twinge of guilt because the basket had been a device to allow her to innocently look around. "It would be lovely. Listen to us talking gardening! My mother says it's a sign you're becoming a middle-aged woman when you become interested in gardening."

"I hope not," Mike said. "I have an English garden in my backyard that I did myself several years ago. I guess I'll have to check and make sure I'm not a middle-aged woman."

Gerry giggled.

"The one with the blue windbreaker and red shirt?" Leslie muttered.

"That's the one," Mike muttered back.

"It's not the guy I saw in Cornwall. But he

turned away, it seemed to me deliberately, when I looked at him."

"He did that twice to me."

"Did what twice?" Gerry asked, clearly overhearing.

"Nothing," Leslie said quickly, not wanting to alarm her. Gerry was fragile enough at the moment. Leslie wasn't about to tell her they might get mugged any minute. That was, if they'd had the bag with them. He'd probably go after it when they got back to the hotel.

"Oh." Gerry blushed, then huffed, "I *see.*"

Leslie realized Gerry thought she and Mike had been talking about intimate things. Mike shrugged, helpless to say anything either. Gerry moved ahead of them slightly, affronted and probably feeling like a third wheel. Leslie couldn't stop the surge of satisfaction inside her, in revenge for Gerry showing up at the worst possible moment. She hated being human like this, but, dammit, hadn't she been left on her own for most of the trip?

Mrs. Wilkens, who had been walking ahead of them, engaged Gerry in conversation. Feeling a little guilty, Leslie promised herself that she'd explain to Gerry once they were out of the group. She sent a silent message of thanks to Mrs. Wilkens for being her chatty self and taking Gerry under her wing. The English were so hospitable.

"Can you see him?" Mike asked in a low voice. "It would be too obvious if I looked."

Leslie casually stopped as if to admire the black-painted timber and pristine white plaster of an Elizabethan town house, now converted into a tearoom. It had a nice big picture window. Her stop made Mike have to stop too. The diamond-shaped panes were small and encased in lead framing, but reflected in the glass, she could make out the people in the group.

"He's not there, I don't think," she said, peering closely. "Can you tell?"

Mike made his own minute examination of the panes. "No."

He turned around and so did she. They scanned the people on the pavement together. The man was nowhere in sight.

"He must have turned off," Leslie said, her heart thumping with excitement at participating in a real-life suspense.

"He was probably just some person trying to crash the tour, and he thought we caught him," Mike said.

"Either that or our hotel room will be burglarized in about fifteen minutes." She glanced up hopefully. "Can we go back now?"

He snorted in amusement. "If I thought we could go back and get in that bed and make love all afternoon and evening, I'd say, 'Hell, yes.' But if that really was our guy, then hell, no, woman, you're not getting any more unsensible than you are already! I'm not putting you in harm's way. If our room's been broken into, we do have our description, which is all that Detective Inspector Lawton wanted in the first place."

Leslie made a face at him.

"Woman, you'll be the death of me yet," he said, then kissed her forehead.

When they returned to their room much later, they found it in the same condition it had been in when they'd left. The carry-on sat undisturbed in the back of the closet.

"Too bad," Leslie said, disappointed nothing had happened. Whoever that young man was, he wasn't involved with their book thieves.

Then she berated herself. Here she was with Mike and she was wasting time over nonsense. Granted, their last days together would be regrettably chaste, but that was all they had. She'd take it, she thought. She had to. Unfortunately she couldn't do anything at the moment, because he was in the bathroom.

Gerry was sitting on her cot, looking like Cinderella after being told she couldn't attend the ball. Leslie felt half sorry for Gerry, who must be feeling like an intruder. But only half sorry, because she was.

Still, she did need to explain what she and Mike had been talking about earlier. Mike came back into the room when she was about halfway through her explanation.

Gerry nodded at the end, then smiled wanly and said, "I think I'll stay in the room tonight and skip the dinner and dance party."

"Are you sure?" Leslie asked, even as hope was building in her chest.

"You're more than welcome to join us," Mike said.

Leslie shot him a quelling glance. Was he crazy or something? He was far too chivalrous, and she would really have to speak to him about that.

"Well . . ." Gerry began.

Leslie shot the quelling look to her. Gerry clammed up, shaking her head.

A soft knock on the door drew their attention. Mike opened it, and Mrs. Wilkens slipped inside. Her smile was about as bright as her yellow print dress.

"Oh, my goodness!" she announced, her eyes wide with speculation as she took in the "three's company" atmosphere of their room. "I had no idea. No idea!"

"Mrs. Wilkens," Leslie said patiently, "Gerry's rooming with us because the hotels are full for the Flower Festival."

"Oh, of course." Her mouth rounded. "I came to tell you . . . It's terrible, just terrible! The hotel is being evacuated! There's been a bomb scare."

"You're kidding!" Leslie exclaimed, immediately terrified for Mike's safety.

"Omigod, omigod, omigod," Gerry wailed, leaping to her feet and spinning around in a circle.

"We'd better get moving," Mike said in a voice that sounded exactly like a schoolteacher's on drill day. He opened the door. "Ladies."

Leslie's fear dampened at his commonsense attitude. She smiled at him, loving him. Loving him. The whole notion of love happening so quickly to her was frightening, but she couldn't stop it, and she didn't want to try. She headed for the closet. "Just a minute."

"Forget the bag, dammit!" Mike snapped as she dragged it out. "Have you lost all common sense?"

"Probably." She straightened and pushed her hair out of her face with her free hand. "I didn't want to leave—"

Mrs. Wilkens was holding a gun, pointing it directly at her. The fluffy woman's face was a mask of hard malevolence. The bright dress never looked more ridiculous, but the hand holding the gun looked extremely steady. Worse, it looked as if it knew exactly what it was doing. So did Mrs. Wilkens.

Ice sank into Leslie's stomach, turning her insides cold. "Mrs. Wilkens!"

"You might want to rethink your ideas of little blue-haired old ladies," Mike said, suddenly very, very still.

Gerry burst into tears.

"Shut up, you stupid girl!" the little blue-haired old lady snapped in a vicious tone. Gerry cut off her hysteria in mid-cry. "I want the bag."

Leslie swallowed and tried to stall. "But there's a bomb scare—"

"I said that to get you out of the room, but you were all so stupid." She waved the gun. "This whole thing has been botched from the beginning. You bloody Americans couldn't even find your way through a birthday party, let alone be where you're supposed to be. We made enough tries at getting the book quietly, so now I have to resort to this. A half-million pounds isn't bloody worth it. The bag."

Leslie glanced at Mike, not daring to wonder what would happen when Mrs. Wilkens discovered there was no book in the bag. "I don't think—"

"That's right, don't think!" Mrs. Wilkens said. "Just pass over the bag."

"Give her the bag," Mike said, staring at her.

Leslie held out the bag.

To her surprise Mrs. Wilkens didn't take it. Instead she said to Mike, "Open the door."

Mike frowned, but he did open the door.

"Charley!" Mrs. Wilkens said.

A slim young man whom Leslie had never seen before slipped into the room. She had the strongest feeling this was her London burglar.

"See if you can do it bloody right this time," Mrs. Wilkens said. "Get the bag."

The man walked past Mike, giving as much space as he could in the cramped room. As he approached, Leslie automatically tightened her fingers on the heavy nylon straps, not wanting to give up the carry-on. It went against every grain in her body to surrender.

The creep, Charley, grinned at her. "That's right. Fight me, bitch."

All of a sudden Mike exploded into action. He seemed to leap through the air, and Mrs. Wilkens squawked, the gun flying from her hand. Charley didn't do more than turn his head at the commotion behind him, when his eyes and tongue bulged, his face turned red. He was lifted off his feet by his collar and shirtback and thrown into the wall. He went down in a shower of plaster. Mike flung himself on top of Charley, pressing his fingers into the man's neck. Charley screamed, then blacked out. Leslie realized Mrs. Wilkens was unguarded, and she threw herself at the older woman, taking them both down in a heap onto the cot, the carry-on still in her hand. Mrs. Wilkens struggled, until it was like trying to pin down a beach ball. Leslie cursed and scrambled to keep her still. How could one little old lady have so much strength?

"Jam your thumb between her neck chords!" Mike shouted.

"No way!" Leslie whapped the woman over the head with the empty carry-on several times. It was enough to take the starch out of Mrs. Wilkens, who finally collapsed under her. Leslie didn't feel the least guilty for resorting to subduing with baggage. Mrs. Wilkens was hardly a sweet little grandmotherly type. She didn't have the gun on a lark, and probably would have used it in an instant.

"That's my girl," Mike said, grinning. "You okay?"

Leslie grinned back. "Fine. Where did you learn all that stuff anyway?"

"Twenty years of Tang Soo Do karate," he said. "My mother made me go, because my body was growing too fast and she hoped I'd acquire some grace of movement. I wound up earning my master's belt." He chuckled. "The occasional jump-front kick and over-shoulder throw comes in handy."

"The things you know," she said in awe. Mrs. Wilkens twitched a little. Leslie glared at her for a second. The woman stilled again.

"I called the front desk," Gerry said, interrupting them. She held up the gun, butt between thumb and forefinger. "What should I do with this?"

"A person of great common sense," Mike said, and congratulated her on having the presence of mind to pick up the gun and call for the authorities. "Just hang on to it for the moment."

"I love you," Leslie said to him. She did. She had from the first moment in that elevator. She knew it now.

"Now you tell me!" he complained, keeping their other burglar subdued. But he grinned. "I love you too."

Leslie smiled happily, knowing she'd completely lost all her common sense.

Gerry was welcome to it.

"I'll be there," Mike said, kissing Leslie soundly at the last stop for nonpassengers at Heathrow Airport, as far as he was allowed to go.

"Of course you will," Leslie said, not a quaver in her voice.

She didn't look apprehensive, but he wasn't reassured. Dammit, he thought. She had to trust in him, and he had to trust she wouldn't panic at their separation. He couldn't believe how fast the trip had ended. They had spent yet another day in a police station, Leslie saying they were old pros at it now. Inspector Lawton had arrived, horrified at his miscalculations but pleased to get the thieves under arrest. Little Old Lady Wilkens, an avid art collector, had been the brains behind the thefts, bored with her wealth and wanting to use her connections to outwit everybody. Their stalker on the tour turned out to be a rookie Yard man, who was being returned to school for more tailing lessons. Mike and Leslie had had only three more days after that.

The first boarding call sounded over the loudspeakers. He knew she still had a walk to the jetway. She had to leave now.

"Twelve weeks," he said, pulling her to him, desperate to transfer his surety to her. "Damn, but I couldn't care less about Jonson now. If this weren't tied to my job, and if I didn't need a job . . ."

She kissed him fervently, her tongue swirling with his in love and promise until Gerry tugged on their arms. They broke away.

"We have to go, Leslie," she said, sounding extremely sensible. She smiled apologetically to soften the blow.

"I know." Leslie looked at him, slowly disengaging from their embrace. "Twelve weeks, or I'll hunt you down."

"Eleven." He kissed her soundly. "I'll wrap it up as soon as I can. Remember the Adams. 'My heart is with you always.' "

Her smile was radiant. "Always."

He let her go, every instinct inside him protesting as she walked through the metal detector and out the other side. She stepped onto a strip walk, allowing it to carry her faster than her feet would. But she was disappearing more quickly than he could bear.

"I love you!" he shouted, not caring about the crowds around him. People laughed and applauded.

"I love you!" she shouted back just as she vanished from his view.

People cheered.

"I hate this," he muttered, shoving his hands in his pants pockets and turning away. He couldn't even wait for her plane to leave, the thought too painful to bear.

"You're taking this very calmly," Gerry said to Leslie a short time later as the plane lifted off British soil.

Leslie looked out at the terminal building. "I am calm. He'll be home in three months, and he'll come to me." She turned to Gerry and smiled. "I *know* it."

"Are you having premonitions now?" Gerry asked in amusement.

Leslie grinned, remembering his last quote. "No. Just a sure thing."

EPILOGUE

"Michael Alfred Smith, you were told not to bring that play snake with you."

Leslie held out her hand to her eldest, eight years old and a typical boy. He was already the tallest one in his class and looked to outshoot even his father in height.

"I'll just keep it in my pocket," he said, trying to bargain with her.

Leslie flicked her fingers in denial. This *was* a Smithsonian Institution ceremony. Michael moaned, but handed over the toy. She gave it to Mike, who was standing beside her. He stopped looking sternly at the child and turned a puzzled frown on her.

"What am I supposed to do with it?" he asked.

She looked heavenward. "Put it in your

pocket, Mike. If he has it, he'll keep taking it out and playing with it. Trust me."

"Oh."

The kids giggled at their father's temporary bewilderment. Leslie smiled indulgently at her husband. Mike was a wonderful husband, but he did revert to temporary losses of sense once in a while. He had managed to weave their special poet, A. E. Housman, through their children's middle names. Young Mike got Alfred, which was only referred to in times of deep discipline. Six-year-old Jeremy's middle name was Edward, and baby Melissa's was Housman. Leslie had told Mike she would not be the one to explain that to Melissa when the child got older. She had tried for Alaric for one of the boys, but Mike wasn't having it. Sometimes she had moments of unsensibility too.

But he had come home to her three months to the day, and they had married two days later in the most unsensible manner. Dogs and cats and lifestyles had blended far more easily than either had expected. Some good had even come out of the separation, with Mike writing a treatise on Jonson and Shakespeare that had earned him a step up in the Literature Department to assistant chairman. Now he was chairman at Rutgers. Their days had a twinge of *Please Don't Eat the Daisies* to it, while their nights were filled with passion. This time she had married against all odds, and it was still an exciting roller-coaster ride that didn't seem to end.

Or maybe she had looked very sensibly into her inner soul this time and found a man of true worth, because it seemed that Mike was the most sensible choice of all. They fit perfectly together in body and spirit.

The curator of the museum stepped up to the small podium, smiling as he announced, "It is my pleasure to unveil our latest acquisition, which was donated by Mrs. Stanforth Peabody in her will. We here at the Smithsonian like to display items that give us a glimpse into the lives of important Americans through the centuries. We're also pleased that this first edition of the first romance novel written is part of the literature display in our Women's Wing. I would also like to thank Professor and Mrs. Michael Smith, who are here with us today. They were instrumental in returning the Adams to Mrs. Peabody several years ago and bringing about this donation."

The small crowd gathered in front of a covered glass case applauded as the curator lifted the velvet away. A book lay open to its dedication page. The Adams was now in a very safe place and would be enjoyed by people for generations to come.

"Too bad Gerry couldn't be here," Leslie said. Gerry was on her honeymoon. It had taken nine years of sensibility, but she had finally found a man who truly cared for her.

"It is," Mike said, "but it was really all your doing, love." He kissed her on the temple. "You saved it from a hidden collection."

"You campaigned for it to be displayed," she reminded him. "As well as saved it."

"Yeah, Dad, you took that guy out." Michael grinned proudly. "And Mom sat on that lady."

Jeremy, the quieter, more solemn son, added, "But Dad was the hero. Mom said."

"Now, that's a quote you can bank on," Mike whispered.

Leslie laughed. "I already did."

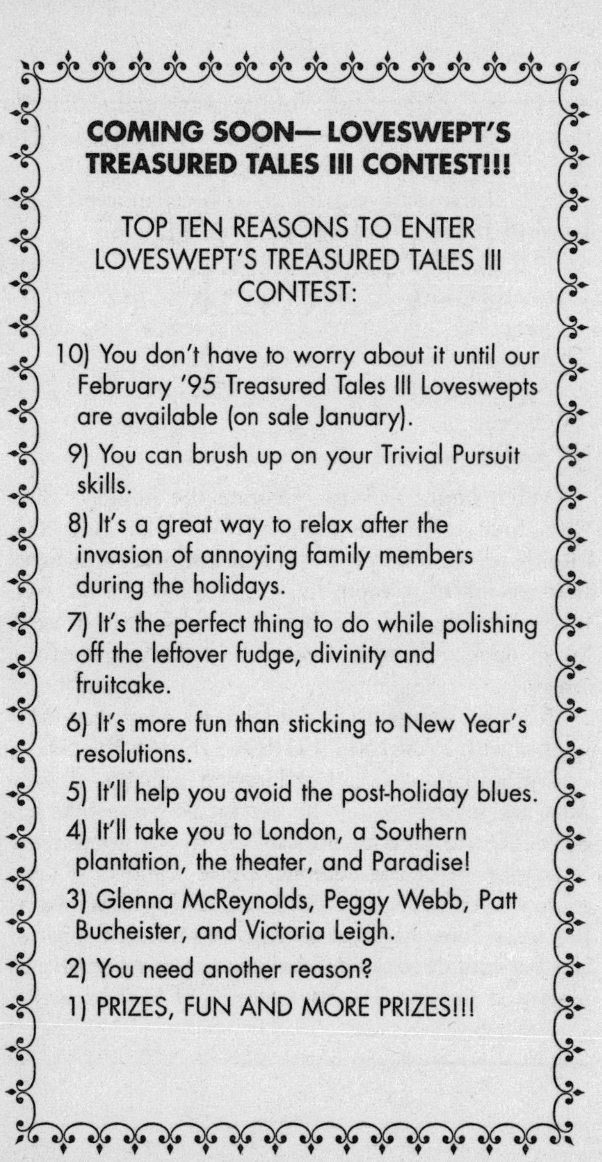

COMING SOON— LOVESWEPT'S TREASURED TALES III CONTEST!!!

TOP TEN REASONS TO ENTER LOVESWEPT'S TREASURED TALES III CONTEST:

10) You don't have to worry about it until our February '95 Treasured Tales III Loveswepts are available (on sale January).

9) You can brush up on your Trivial Pursuit skills.

8) It's a great way to relax after the invasion of annoying family members during the holidays.

7) It's the perfect thing to do while polishing off the leftover fudge, divinity and fruitcake.

6) It's more fun than sticking to New Year's resolutions.

5) It'll help you avoid the post-holiday blues.

4) It'll take you to London, a Southern plantation, the theater, and Paradise!

3) Glenna McReynolds, Peggy Webb, Patt Bucheister, and Victoria Leigh.

2) You need another reason?

1) PRIZES, FUN AND MORE PRIZES!!!

THE EDITOR'S CORNER

What better way to celebrate the holidays than with four terrific new LOVESWEPTs! And this month we are excited to present you with romances that are full of passion, humor, and most of all, true love—everything that is best about this time of year. So sit back and indulge yourself in the magic of the season.

Starting things off is the fabulous Mary Kay McComas with **PASSING THROUGH MIDNIGHT**, LOVESWEPT #722. Gil Howlett believes all women are mysteries, but he *has* to discover what has driven Dorie Devries into hiding in his hometown! Struggling with old demons, Dorie wonders if deep sorrow ever heals, but Gil's tenderness slowly wins her trust. Now he must soothe the wounded spirit of this big-city doctor who challenges him to believe in forgotten dreams. Heartwarming and heartbreaking,

Mary Kay's novels weave a marvelous tapestry of emotions into stories you wish would never end.

The wonderfully talented Debra Dixon wants to introduce you to **DOC HOLIDAY**, LOVESWEPT #723. Drew Haywood needs an enchantress to help give his son a holiday to remember—and no one does Christmas better than Taylor Bishop! She can transform a house into a home that smells of gingerbread and sparkles with tinsel, and kissing her is like coming out of the cold. She's spent her whole life caring for others, but when sweet temptation beckons, this sexy family man must convince her to break all her rules. With poignant humor and sizzling sensuality, Debra has crafted an unforgettable story of the magic of Christmas.

The ever-popular Adrienne Staff returns with **SPELLBOUND**, LOVESWEPT #724. Edward Rockford sees her first in the shadows and senses the pretty artist somehow holds the key to his secrets—but when he enters Jamie Payton's loft, he is stunned to discover that her painting reveals what he's hidden from all the world. Haunted by ghosts from the past, Jamie yearns to share his sanctuary. But can his seductive sorcery set her free? Conjured of equal parts destiny and mystery, passion and emotion, Adrienne's stories capture the imagination and compel the heart to believe once more in a love for all time.

Last but never least is Susan Connell with **RINGS ON HER FINGERS**, LOVESWEPT #725. She really knows how to fill her Christmas stockings, Steve Stratton decides with admiration at first sight of the long-legged brunette dressed as a holiday elf! Gwen Mansfield feels her heart racing like a runaway sleigh when the gorgeous architect invites her to play under his tree—and vows to be good. A jinxed love life has made her wary, but maybe Steve is the one to change her luck. Susan Connell has always written about intrepid heroes and damsels in just enough distress to make life interesting, but now she delivers the perfect Christmas present, complete with surprises and glittering fun!

Happy reading!

With best wishes,

Beth de Guzman

Senior Editor

P.S. Don't miss the exciting women's novels that are coming your way from Bantam in January! **HEAVEN'S PRICE,** from blockbuster author Sandra Brown, is a classic romantic novel in hardcover for the first time; **LORD OF ENCHANTMENT,** by bestselling author Suzanne Robinson, is an enchanting tale of romance and intrigue on a stormy isle off the coast of Elizabethan England; **SURRENDER TO A STRANGER,** by Karyn Monk, is an utterly compelling, passionately romantic debut from an exceptionally talented new historical romance author. We'll be giving you a sneak peek at these terrific books in next month's LOVESWEPTs. And immediately following this page look for a preview of the exciting romances from Bantam that are *available now!*

Don't miss these sensational books by your favorite Bantam authors

On sale in November

ADAM'S FALL
by Sandra Brown

PURE SIN
by Susan Johnson

ON WINGS OF MAGIC
by Kay Hooper

ADAM'S FALL

by

SANDRA BROWN

"Ms. Brown's larger than life heroes and heroines make you believe all the warm, wonderful, wild things in life."
—*Rendezvous*

BLOCKBUSTER AUTHOR SANDRA BROWN—WHOSE NAME IS ALMOST SYNONYMOUS WITH *THE NEW YORK TIMES* BEST-SELLER LIST—OFFERS A CLASSIC ROMANTIC NOVEL THAT ACHES WITH EMOTION AND SIZZLES WITH PASSION. . . .

They still fought like cats and dogs, but their relationship drastically improved.

He still cursed her, accused her of being heartless out of pure meanness, and insisted that she pushed him beyond his threshold of pain and endurance.

She still cursed him and accused him of being a

gutless rich kid who, for the first time in his charmed life, was experiencing hardship.

He said she couldn't handle patients worth a damn.

She said he couldn't handle adversity worth a damn.

He said she taunted him unmercifully.

She said he whined incessantly.

And so it went. But things were definitely better.

He came to trust her just a little. He began to listen when she told him that he wasn't trying hard enough and should put more concentration into it. And he listened when she advised that he was trying too hard and needed to rest awhile.

"Didn't I tell you so?" She was standing at the foot of his bed, giving therapy to his ankle.

"I'm still not ready to tap dance."

"But you've got sensation."

"You stuck a straight pin into my big toe!"

"But you've got sensation." She stopped turning his foot and looked up toward the head of his bed, demanding that he agree.

"I've got sensation." The admission was grumbled, but he couldn't hide his pleased smile.

"In only two and a half weeks." She whistled. "You've come a long way, baby. I'm calling Honolulu today and ordering a set of parallel bars. You'll soon be able to stand between them."

His smile collapsed. "I'll never be able to do that."

"That's what you said about the wheelchair. Will you lighten up?"

"Will you?" He grunted with pain as she bent his knee back toward his chest.

"Not until you're walking."

"If you keep wearing those shorts, I'll soon be running. I'll be chasing you."

"Promises, promises."

"I thought I told you to dress more modestly."

"This is Hawaii, Cavanaugh. Everybody goes casual, or haven't you heard? I'm going to resist the movement now. Push against my hand. That's it. A little harder. Good."

"Ah, God," he gasped through clenched teeth. He followed her instructions, which took him through a routine to stretch his calf muscle. "The backs of your legs are sunburned," he observed as he put forth even greater effort.

"You noticed?"

"How could I help it? You flash them by me every chance you get. Think those legs of yours are long enough? They must start in your armpits. But how'd I get off on that? What were we talking about?"

"Why my legs were sunburned. Okay, Adam, let up a bit, then try it again. Come on now, no ugly faces. One more time." She picked up the asinine conversation in order to keep his mind off his discomfort. "My legs are sunburned because I fell asleep beside the pool yesterday afternoon."

"Is that what you're being paid an exorbitant amount of money to do? To nap beside my swimming pool?"

"Of course not!" After a strategic pause, she added, "I went swimming too." He gave her a baleful look and pressed his foot against the palm of her hand. "Good, Adam, good. Once more."

"You said that was the last one."
"I lied."
"You heartless bitch."
"You gutless preppy."
Things were swell.

"Susan Johnson brings sensuality to new heights and beyond."
—*Romantic Times*

Susan Johnson

NATIONALLY BESTSELLING AUTHOR OF *SEIZED BY LOVE* AND *OUTLAW*

PURE SIN

From the erotic imagination of bestselling author Susan Johnson comes a tale of exquisite pleasure that begins in the wilds of Montana—and ends in the untamed places of two lovers' hearts.

"A shame we didn't ever meet," Adam said with a seductive smile, his responses automatic with beautiful women. "Good conversation is rare."

She didn't suppose most women were interested exclusively in his conversation, Flora thought, as she took in the full splendor of his dark beauty and power. Even lounging in a chair, his legs casually crossed at the ankles, he presented an irresistible image of brute strength. And she'd heard enough rumor in the course of the evening to understand he enjoyed women—nonconversationally. "As rare as marital fidelity no doubt."

His brows rose fractionally. "No one's had the nerve to so bluntly allude to my marriage. Are you speaking of Isolde's or my infidelities?" His grin was boyish.

"Papa says you're French."

"Does that give me motive or excuse? And I'm only half French, as you no doubt know, so I may have less excuse than Isolde. She apparently prefers Baron Lacretelle's properties in Paris and Nice to my dwelling here."

"No heartbroken melancholy?"

He laughed. "Obviously you haven't met Isolde."

"Why did you marry then?"

He gazed at her for a moment over the rim of the goblet he'd raised to his lips. "You can't be that naive," he softly said, then quickly drained the glass.

"Forgive me. I'm sure it's none of my business."

"I'm sure it's not." The warmth had gone from his voice and his eyes. Remembering the reason he'd married Isolde always brought a sense of chaffing anger.

"I haven't felt so gauche in years," Flora said, her voice almost a whisper.

His black eyes held hers, their vital energy almost mesmerizing, then his look went shuttered and his grin reappeared. "How could you know, darling? About the idiosyncrasies of my marriage. Tell me now about your first sight of Hagia Sophia."

"It was early in the morning," she began, relieved he'd so graciously overlooked her faux pas. "The sun had just begun to appear over the crest of the—"

"Come dance with me," Adam abruptly said, leaning forward in his chair. "This waltz is a favorite of mine," he went on, as though they hadn't been discussing something completely different. Reaching over, he took her hands in his. “And I’ve been wanting to”—his hesitation was minute as he discarded the inappropriate verb—“hold you.” He grinned. “You see how blandly circumspect my choice of words is.” Rising, he gently pulled her to her feet. “Considering the newest scandal in my life, I’m on my best behavior tonight.”

“But then scandals don’t bother me.” She was standing very close to him, her hands still twined in his.

His fine mouth, only inches away, was graced with a genial smile and touched with a small heated playfulness. “I thought they might not.”

“When one travels as I do, one becomes inured to other people’s notions of nicety.” Her bare shoulders lifted briefly, ruffling the limpid lace on her décolletage. He noticed both the pale satin of her skin and the tantalizing swell of her bosom beneath the delicate lace. “If I worried about scandal,” she murmured with a small smile, “I’d never set foot outside England.”

“And you do.”

“Oh yes,” she whispered. And for a moment both were speaking of something quite different.

“You’re not helping,” he said in a very low voice. “I’ve sworn off women for the moment.”

“To let your wounds heal?”

“Nothing so poetical.” His quirked grin reminded her of a teasing young boy. “I’m reassessing my priorities.”

“Did I arrive in Virginia City too late then?”

“Too late?” One dark brow arched infinitesimally.

“To take advantage of your former priorities.”

He took a deep breath because he was already perversely aware of the closeness of her heated body, of the heady fragrance of her skin. "You're a bold young lady, Miss Bonham."

"I'm twenty-six years old, Mr. Serre, and independent."

"I'm not sure after marriage to Isolde that I'm interested in any more willful aristocratic ladies."

"Perhaps I could change your mind."

He thoughtfully gazed down at her, and then the faintest smile lifted the graceful curve of his mouth. "Perhaps you could."

"[Kay Hooper] writes with exceptional beauty and grace."
—*Romantic Times*

Kay Hooper

NATIONALLY BESTSELLING AUTHOR OF
THE WIZARD OF SEATTLE

ON WINGS OF MAGIC

One of today's most beloved romance authors, Kay Hooper captivates readers with the wit and sensuality of her work. Now the award-winning writer offers a passionate story filled with all the humor and tenderness her fans have come to expect—a story that explores the loneliness of heartbreak and the searing power of love. . . .

"Tell me, Kendall—why the charade?"

"Why not?" She looked at him wryly. "I am what people expect me to be."

"You mean men."

"Sure. Oh, I could rant and rave about not being valued for who I am instead of what I look like, but what good would that do? My way is much easier. And there's no harm done."

"I don't know about that." Seriously, he went on, "By being what people expect you to be, you don't give anyone the chance to see the real you."

Interested in spite of herself, she frowned thoughtfully. "But how many people really care what's beneath the surface, Hawke? Not many," she went on, answering her own question. "We all act out roles we've given ourselves, pretend to be things we're not—or things we want to be. And we build walls around the things we want to hide."

"What do you want to hide, Kendall?" he asked softly.

Ignoring the question, she continued calmly. "It's human nature. We want to guess everyone else's secrets without giving our own away."

"And if someone wants to see beneath the surface?"

Kendall shrugged. "We make them dig for it. You know—make them prove themselves worthy of our trust. Of all the animals on this earth, we're the most suspicious of a hand held out in friendship."

Hawke pushed his bowl away and gazed at her with an oddly sober gleam in his eyes. "Sounds like you learned that lesson the hard way," he commented quietly.

She stared at him, surprise in her eyes, realizing for the first time just how cynical she'd become. Obeying some nameless command in his smoky eyes, she said slowly, "I've seen too much to be innocent, Hawke. Whatever ideals I had . . . died long ago."

He stared at her for a long moment, then murmured, "I think I'd better find a pick and a shovel."

Suddenly angry with her own burst of self-revelation, Kendall snapped irritably, "Why?"

"To dig beneath the surface." He smiled slowly. "You're a fascinating lady, Kendall James. And I think

. . . if I dig deep enough . . . I just might find gold."

"What you might find," she warned coolly, "is a booby trap. I'm not a puzzle to be solved, Hawke."

"Aren't you? You act the sweet innocent, telling yourself that it's the easy way. And it's a good act, very convincing and probably very useful. But it isn't entirely an act, is it, honey? There is an innocent inside of you, hiding from the things she's seen."

"You're not a psychologist and I'm not a patient, so stop with the analyzing," she muttered, trying to ignore what he was saying.

"You're a romantic, an idealist," he went on as if she hadn't spoken. "But you hide that part of your nature—behind a wall that isn't a wall at all. You've got yourself convinced that it's an act, and that conviction keeps you from being hurt."

Kendall shot him a glare from beneath her lashes. "Now you're not even making sense," she retorted scornfully.

"Oh, yes, I am." His eyes got that hooded look she was beginning to recognize out of sheer self-defense. "A piece of the puzzle just fell into place. But it's still a long way from being solved. And, rest assured, Kendall, I intend to solve it."

"Is this in the nature of another warning?" she asked lightly, irritated that her heart had begun to beat like a jungle drum.

"Call it anything you like."

"I could just leave, you know."

"You could." The heavy lids lifted, revealing a cool challenge. "But that would be cowardly."

Knowing—*knowing*—that she was walking right

into his trap, Kendall snapped, "I'm a lot of things, Hawke, but a coward isn't one of them!" And felt strongly tempted to throw her soup bowl at him when she saw the satisfaction that flickered briefly in his eyes.

"Good," he said briskly. "Then we can forget about that angle, can't we? And get down to business."

"Business?" she murmured wryly. "That's one I haven't heard."

"Well, I would have called it romance, but I didn't want you to laugh at me." He grinned faintly. "Men are more romantic than women, you know. I read it somewhere."

"Fancy that." Kendall stared at him. "Most of the men I've known let romance go by the board."

"Really? Then knowing me will be an education."

And don't miss these wonderful romances from Bantam Books, on sale in December:

HEAVEN'S PRICE

by the *New York Times* bestselling author

Sandra Brown

a new hardcover edition of the Sandra Brown classic!

LORD OF ENCHANTMENT

by the nationally bestselling

Suzanne Robinson

"An author with star quality . . . spectacularly talented."

—*Romantic Times*

SURRENDER TO A STRANGER

by the highly talented

Karyn Monk

When a stranger risks everything to rescue a proud beauty, she owes him her life, her heart—and her soul. . . .

Don't miss these fabulous Bantam women's fiction titles

Now On Sale

ADAM'S FALL

by *New York Times* bestselling author

Sandra Brown

Blockbuster author Sandra Brown—whose name is almost synonymous with the *New York Times* bestseller list—offers a classic romantic novel that aches with emotion and sizzles with passion.

❑ *56768-3 $4.99/$5.99 in Canada*

PURE SIN

by nationally bestselling author

Susan Johnson

From the erotic imagination of Susan Johnson comes a tale of exquisite pleasure that begins in the wilds of Montana—and ends in the untamed places of two lovers' hearts.

❑ *29956-5 $5.50/6.99 in Canada*

ON WINGS OF MAGIC

by award-winning author

Kay Hooper

Award-winning Kay Hooper offers a passionate story filled with all the humor and tenderness her fans have come to expect—a story that explores the loneliness of heartbreak and the searing power of love.

❑ *56965-1 $4.99/$5.99 in Canada*

Ask for these books at your local bookstore or use this page to order.

❑ Please send me the books I have checked above. I am enclosing $ ______ (add $2.50 to cover postage and handling). Send check or money order, no cash or C. O. D.'s, please.

Name ____________________

Address ____________________

City/ State/ Zip ____________________

Send order to: Bantam Books, Dept. FN156, 2451 S. Wolf Rd., Des Plaines, IL 60018

Allow four to six weeks for delivery.

Prices and availability subject to change without notice. FN156 12/94